The Unbeheaded King

Volume Three of **The Reluctant King**

L. Sprague de Camp

A Del Rey Book

BALLANTINE BOOKS • NEW YORK

CONTENTS

I

THE PALACE OF XYLAR

A LARGE COPPER BATHTUB, ITS POLISHED SURFACE REDLY reflecting the light of the setting sun, soared above the snow-clad peaks of the Lograms. It wove around the loftiest summits and scraped over the lower ones, betimes with but a few cubits to spare.

"Gorax!" yelled one of the two men in the tub. "I have commanded thee not to miss those peaks so straitly! Wouldst stop my old heart from sheer fright? Next time, go around!"

"What's his answer?" asked the other man.

The first cocked his head as if listening. At last he spoke: "He says he is fain to get this journey over with. He also begs that I suffer him to alight on one of these mountains to rest; but I know better. Did I permit him, his last labor for me were completed. Away the fiend would flit to his native dimension, leaving us stranded on an icy mountain top."

The speaker was a small, lean, brown-skinned man in a coarse brown robe. The wind of the tub's motion rippled the silky white hair that hung down beneath his bulbous white turban and fluttered his vast white beard. He was Karadur, a seer and wizard from Mulvan.

The other tub-rider was a large man in late youth, with a ruddy complexion further reddened by the mountain winds, deep-set dark eyes and black hair and beard, and a scar across his face that put a slight kink in his nose. This was Jorian of Ardamai in Kortoli, once King of Xylar and, before and since, a poet, mercenary soldier, professional taleteller, bookkeeper, clockmaker, and surveyor.

Continuing an argument that had begun before they narrowly missed the mountain peak, Karadur said: "But, my son! To rush unprepared into such an adventure were a sure formula for disaster. We should instruct Gorax to set us down in some safe land, where we have friends, and plan our next move."

"By the time we've done planning," said Jorian, "the Xylarians will have gotten word of my flight from Penembei. I know, because when I was King, the secret service was on its toes. Then they will set traps for me, hoping I'll try to rescue Estrildis. And then...."

Jorian brought the edge of his hand sharply against his neck. He alluded to the bloody Xylarian custom of cutting off the king's head every five years and throwing it up for grabs, the catcher to be the next king. Karadur's magic had enabled Jorian to escape his own beheading. Ever since, Xylar had sought to recapture its fugitive king, to drag him back and resume their interrupted ceremony so that his successor could be chosen in the time-honored way.

"Besides," Jorian continued, "so long as Gorax remains your slave, we have this aerial vehicle to approach the palace from aloft. You yourself said that, if you permit him to alight, that were the end of his services. Any earthbound attempt were rendered that much harder. Why think you I brought this along?" He pointed to the coil of rope lying at one end of King Ishbahar's tub. "Could you magic that rope as you did the one in Xylar?"

Karadur shook his head. "Alas, nay! It requires the capture of a spirit from the Second Plane, for which I have no present facilities." Then Karadur tried another tack. In his high, nasal voice, he droned on: "But Jorian dear! The world harbors many attractive women. Why must you remain fixated upon this one? She is a nice girl; but you have enjoyed many women, both during your kingship and since. So it is not as if she were the only possible mate—"

"I've told you before," growled Jorian, "she's the one I chose myself. Those other four wives were picked for me by the Regency Council. Nought wrong with them; but 'twas an arrangement political. What would an ascetic old sage like you know of love?"

"You forget that I, too, was once young, difficult though you may find that to believe."

"Well, if King Fusinian of Kortoli could risk his life to rescue his beloved Thanuda from the troll Vuum, I were a recreant knave not to make an effort."

"There are still those other women of whom you have had carnal knowledge since your escape."

"You can't blame me about the high priestess. I had little choice in that matter."

"Aye; but there were others—"

Jorian snorted. "I try to be faithful to Estrildis; but I'm not yet able, after long abstinence, calmly to dismiss unplumbed a fair lass who crawls into bed with me, begging that I pleasure her. When I reach your age, perhaps my self-control will be equal to the challenge."

Karadur said: "How know you the Xylarians have not bestowed your Estrildis upon another?"

"They hadn't when my brother Kerin was there, repairing their clocks. I suspect they save her as bait for me. Through Kerin, I got word to her to hold out."

"Suppose her affections prove less perdurable than yours? Suppose she, too, has found agreeable the company of another of the opposite sex?"

"Ridiculous!" snapped Jorian. "She always told me I was her true love, and I trust her as far as I trust any mortal."

"Ah, but ofttimes Astis—the goddess whom we in Mulvan call Laxari—afflicts the steadiest of mortals with a passion that overrides the weightiest resolves and the most cogent reasonings. Misprize not the havoc that fate and the vagaries of human nature can make with our soberest plans. As said the wise Cidam, 'Blessed be he who expecteth the worst, for verily he shall ne'er be disappointed.'"

Jorian scowled. "You mean, let's suppose she has willingly suffered some knave to mount her in my absence? I suppose it could happen. Since I was the best swordsman in Xylar, excepting Tartonio, the fencing master who taught me, I should easily skewer the villain. Some would say to slay the woman, too, but I'm too chicken-hearted."

"You say you love her, right?"

"Aye, desperately."

"Then you would fain not wantonly render her unhappy, would you?"

"Of course not!"

"But suppose she really love this wight? Then you had broken her heart to no purpose. If by force or fraud you compelled her to live with you thereafter, your domestic scene were something less than heavenly."

Jorian shook his head. "Curse it, old man, but you think of some of the direst predicaments! Whatever I propose, you are endlessly fertile in reasons why it were a folly, a blunder, and a wicked knavery. Betimes you have reason; but if I harkened to all your cavils, I'd stand immobile until I sprouted roots. Methinks I must await the event and guide my actions accordingly."

Karadur sighed. "It is difficult for one so young to take the long view of what is best for all concerned."

Jorian glanced up. Overhead the stars were coming out. "Pray tell your demon to go slowly. We would not run into Mount Aravia in the dark."

"Mount Aravia? I believe a colleague of mine, named Shenderu, dwells there as a wise hermit. Could we not pay him a visit?" At Jorian's expression, Karadur sighed again. "Nay, I suppose not."

A scarlet-and-golden dawn found the flying bathtub still over the Lograms, although the ridges became lower as

4

the travelers flew northward. Soon the mountains ended, and for hours they soared above the vast Marshes of Moru. This dubious place was nominally part of Xylar. In practice it was a no-man's land, inhabited by a few desperate men, by dwarf crocodiles, and, it was rumored, by descendants of the dragons that the cannibal Paaluans once brought to Novaria. Generations before, these sophisticated cannibals sent a foraging expedition to Ir on the west coast of the broad Novarian peninsula.

Curious about everything, Jorian peered over the side of the tub. He looked in vain for a Paaluan dragon among the black pools and gray-green tussocks of this everglade, whence the approach of winter had bleached most of the color. Karadur cautioned:

"Lean not so far, my son! Gorax complains that you rock the tub and might overset it, despite his endeavors to fly it on an even keel."

"The tub has no keel," grinned Jorian. "But I get his point."

"Two gentlemen fleeing away
From warfare in doomed Penembei,
    Their carriage capsized,
    The marsh fertilized;
Their bones molder there to this day!"

"Not your best, my son," said Karadur. "We know not whether Penembei in fact be doomed. If that fellow Chuivir, whom you nominated king, make good his claim, he may prove a good-to-middling monarch. Besides, methinks you require a conjunction at the beginning of that last line."

"That would spoil the meter," said Jorian. "The first foot should always be an iamb, according to Doctor Gwiderius."

"Who?"

"The professor who taught me prosody at the Academy of Othomae. Well, how's this?"

"Two knaves in the royal washbasin
O'er Moru's dank marshes did hasten,
But leaning too far,
They fell with a jar,
And mud their presumption did chasten."

Karadur shook his head. "That implies that I, too, am leaning over the side. As you can perceive, I am careful to keep to the centerline."

"What a literal-minded gaffer you are! All right, let's see you compose a better!"

"Alas, Jorian, I am no poet; nor is Novarian my native tongue. To compose a verse incorporating the thoughts of yours in Mulvani, and obeying all sixty-three rules of Mulvanian versification, were a task requiring more comfort and leisure than the gods see fit at the moment to accord us."

By afternoon they had left the Marshes of Moru and soared above the forests of southern Xylar. By sunset the forest was giving way to farmland.

"Tell Gorax," said Jorian, "that we do not wish to arrive at Xylar City before midnight."

"He says we shall be fortunate to arrive ere dawn," said Karadur. "He groans—mentally of course—with fatigue."

"Then have him speed up. The last thing we wish is to find the sun rising just as I am shinnying down that rope."

"Just what do you intend, Jorian?" Karadur's voice expressed a growing tremor of apprehension.

"Simple. Kerin told me they have Estrildis quartered in the penthouse apartment on the roof. They think that putting her up there will make it harder for me to get her—assuming that I shall approach the palace on the ground." Jorian chuckled. "So, when we reach the roof, I'll belay the rope to the faucet, drop the other end over the side, slide down, and carry off Estrildis before any mouse knows I'm there. I wish we had one of your ensorcelled ropes."

"If we ever alight long enough for the sorcerous operation, I will prepare one."

"This faucet was King Ishbahar's pride and joy," said Jorian. "An engineer in the House of Learning invented it. The only trouble was that the king's servants had to mix hot and cold water in a tank on the palace roof, and they could never get the proportions right. Poor Ishbahar was ever being either chilled or boiled. I proposed that he install two faucets, one for hot water and one for cold, so that he could adjust the mixture to suit himself. But, what with the siege of Iraz and the revolt of the racing factions, he never got around to trying my idea."

Karadur shook his head. "With all these new inventions pouring out of the House of Learning, in a few centuries our plane will be like the afterworld, where all is done by buzzing, clattering machines and magic is of no account. I pray never to spend an incarnation in such a world."

Jorian shrugged. "I try to make the best of things, be they magical or mechanical. At least we can thank King Ishbahar's monstrous fatness that we have so huge a tub, wherein the twain of us can comfortably sleep. Didst ever hear how he came to have it made?"

"Nay, my son. Tell me, pray."

"When Ishbahar acceded to the throne, he was already vastly obese, eating having been his favorite pastime from boyhood on. Well, the night following his coronation, he was, naturally, weary after a day of standing about and making ceremonial motions and uttering prescribed responses to the high priests of the leading cults. So he commanded his lackeys to prepare a bath for him, and told his favorite wife to await him in the royal bed.

"The royal bathtub, however, had been made for his predecessor, Shashtai the Eighth, who was a small, spare man. Ishbahar tested the water with his finger and found it just right. With a sigh of happy anticipation, he mounted the step that the lackeys had placed beside the tub and lowered himself into the water. But alas! As he sank down, he found himself firmly wedged between the sides of the tub. He called out to a servant: 'Ho, this won't do! We are

7

squeezed to a jelly! Help us out, pray!' So the servitor caught the king's arm and heaved, but without effect. Between the king's vast weight and the wedging effect of the sloping sides of the tub, Ishbahar was stuck fast.

"They called more servants, and all together heaved on the king's arms—to no avail. A guardsman was called, to thrust the butt of his halberd over the edge of the tub and under the royal arse, to pry him up. Ishbahar bore the pain bravely except for a few groans, but still he remained stuck. Then two flunkeys added their weight to that of the guardsman on the head end of the halberd, but they only succeeded in breaking the spear shaft.

"Then the king had the chief engineer of the School of Matter in the House of Learning dragged out of bed. The engineer looked over the problem and told the king: 'Your Majesty, I can get you out. All we need do is bore a hole in the ceiling and install a hoist with compound pulleys. By looping ropes under your armpits and thighs, we shall have you out in a jiffy.'

"'How long will this take?' asked King Ishbahar.

"The engineer thought a moment and said: 'May it please Your Majesty, allowing time for drawing up a plan and assembling materials, I am sure we can have you out in a fortnight.'

"'And meanwhile we shall sit here soaking?' said Ishbahar. 'Come, come, my good fellow! Fetch us the head of the School of Spirit.'

"So they brought in the head wizard of the School of Spirit, a bitter rival of the chief engineer in the House of Learning. The enchanter said: 'Your Majesty, I have just the thing! It is my newly developed levitation spell, which can easily handle up to three talents avoirdupois. Let me fetch my instruments, and all shall be well.'

"So, after midnight, the wizard ordered all the others out of the bath chamber and began his spell. He burned mysterious powders in a brazier, whence arose many-hued smokes that writhed and twined like ghostly serpents. He chanted mystical phrases, and shadows chased each other about the walls, albeit there was no solid body in the chamber to cast them. The hangings rippled, and the can-

8

dle flames flickered, although there was no wind in the chamber.

"At length the wizard cried three words of power, and King Ishbahar rose—but the tub rose with him, still firmly attached to the royal haunches. At length the wizard was compelled by sheer fatigue to let the king and his tub settle back to the floor. This tub, you understand, had no faucet and no pipes to let water in and out, so it could be freely moved.

"At length the favorite wife, named Haziran, came in to see what was keeping her lord so long. She found the king still in the tub, and the chief engineer and the chief wizard and the servants all standing about, muttering disconsolately at their failure to get the king unstuck. They were proposing desperate expedients, such as starving the king until he shrank enough no longer to fit so snugly, like a cork in a bottle.

"Haziran looked the situation over and said, 'You are all a pack of fools! This is a ceramic tub, is it not? Well, you lackeys, take the water out. Doctor Akraba—' That was the chief engineer. '—fetch me a heavy hammer, forthwith!'

"'Do as she says,' quoth Ishbahar. 'This damned tub is cutting off our circulation.'

"By the time the sledge hammer was brought, the servants, with dippers and pails and sponges, had removed nearly all the water. So Haziran smote the tub on the side where it gripped Ishbahar's hips, and with a loud crash the tub broke into several pieces. The king gave a yelp of pain from the impact, but he recked that a bruised hip were a small price for his freedom. He dried himself, embraced Haziran, and led her off to the bedchamber. She was a level-headed woman, and had she not died of a pox a few years later, she might have saved the kingdom much grief by giving Ishbahar good advice.

"Anyway, the king ordered another bathtub. This time he made sure it was large enough so that, no matter how fat he got, he would be in no danger of being entrapped. And in later years, when officials of the House of Learning complained of the king's cutting their appropriations, Ishbahar would say: 'Ha! For all your pretended wisdom, you geniuses could not even get us out of a bathtub!'"

"An edifying tale," said Karadur. "But why did he have it fabricated of copper? It must have been much more costly that way."

"That was a decision political. His officials were embroiled in a quarrel with the potters' guild over taxes, and ordering the tub from the coppersmiths' guild was Ishbahar's way of reminding the potters who was boss."

"Now back to our own plans," said Karadur. "How shall you get your queen up the rope and into the tub again? Mighty though you be, I misdoubt you could scale the rope with one hand whilst grasping your sweetling with the other."

Jorian frowned. "You have a point. I suppose the best way were to have her grasp me round the neck from behind, thus leaving my hands free."

"Do you ween you can hoist the weight of the twain of you?"

"If not, I shall have to remain clinging to the rope until you find us a safe place to alight."

"You cannot dangle until we are out of Xylar! The journey would require hours. And if we alight ere departing this land, Gorax will desert us, and we shall be forced to flee afoot."

"Hmm." After a moment of silence, Jorian said: "I know! There's a ruined castle, said to be haunted, a dozen leagues southeast of Xylar City. A certain Baron Lorc built it back in feudal days. Much of the main wall still stands. Gorax can drop us on the wall and then bring the tub down to the level of the parapet, so we can climb in. Be sure to tell him not to let the tub touch the wall, lest he deem himself freed from his last labor."

Karadur muttered: "I like it not. Demons are tricky beings, especially those we cannot see. And what is this about the castle's being haunted?"

"Just a rumor, a legend. There's probably nought to it; and if a malevolent spirit does abide there, I trust you to protect us from it by magical means."

Karadur dubiously wagged his beard. "Why not bring the tub to the edge of the palace roof, as you speak of doing at Baron Lorc's castle?"

"Because, save for a narrow walk around the penthouse and a little terrace, the roof slopes down on both sides, and there is nought to hang on to ere one reaches the eaves. By myself, I might chance sliding down the roof tiles and leaping into the tub, but I cannot ask that of Estrildis."

"Curse it, boy, could you not take me across the border into Othomae and leave me there? I would instruct Gorax to obey you until his final dismissal."

"Oh, no indeed!" said Jorian. "I need you to control this aerial chariot whilst I am below fetching my darling. Cheer up, old man! We've gotten each other out of more parlous plights."

"All very well for you, young master," grumbled Karadur. "You are constructed of steel springs and whalebone, but I am old and fragile. I know not how many more of these exploits I can endure ere joining the majority."

"Well, you can't complain that life in my company has been dull, now can you?"

"Nay. Betimes I lust for some nice, quiet, boresome dullness."

The time was past midnight and a silvery half-moon was rising when Jorian sighted a sprinkling of faint lights, far off to their left. He said: "Methinks that's Xylar City yonder. Tell our demon, hard to port! His deduced reckoning was off by half a league."

The tub changed course in obedience to the Mulvanian's mental command. Soon the lights grew and multiplied. Some came from the windows of houses; some from the oil lamps that Jorian, when king, had erected on posts at major street crossings. This was the city's first regular street lighting; before, citizens, unless rich enough to hire bodyguards and link boys, stayed home behind bolted doors at night.

"We must keep our voices down," whispered Jorian.

By whispered commands to Karadur, who passed them on mentally to Gorax, Jorian guided the tub to the royal palace. He circled the structure before coming close to the penthouse.

"No guards on the roof; good!" he murmured.

He brought the tub to a halt six cubits above the small square terrace at one end of the penthouse. While Karadur placed the tub just where Jorian wanted it, Jorian knotted one end of the rope around the faucet and dropped the rest over the side. He prepared to climb down.

"No sword?" whispered Karadur.

"Nay. It would clank, or bang the furniture, and give me away. If an alarum sound and the guards rush in, one sword were of no avail against several."

"In the epics," mused Karadur, "heroes are ever slaying a hundred fierce foes single-handed."

"Such tales are lies, as anyone who has done real sword fighting knows. Take a legendary hero like Dauric—but here I am talking when I should be acting."

"Your besetting weakness, my son. That runaway tongue will yet be our doom."

"Perhaps; but there are worse vices than garrulity. The reason I talk so much—"

"Jorian!" said Karadur with unusual vehemence. "*Shut up!*"

Silenced at last, Jorian went over the side and down the rope. The soles of his boots made scarcely a whisper as they touched the tiles of the terrace.

He stole to the door of the penthouse, feeling in his purse for his picklocks. He had learned to use these implements during the year preceding his escape from Xylar. A wise woman had prophesied that Jorian was best fitted to be either king or a wandering adventurer. He had no special desire to be either, since his real ambition was to be a prosperous, respectable craftsman like his father, Evor the Clockmaker. But circumstances conspired to thrust him into these rôles willy-nilly.

Jorian had become King of Xylar by unintentionally catching the head of his predecessor when it was thrown from the execution scaffold. Since it was plain that he could not indefinitely continue as king in the face of the Xylarian law of succession, he had determined to be the ablest adventurer he could. So he had trained himself for the rôle as rationally and thoroughly as would any expert in science, art, or law.

He studied languages, practiced martial arts, and hired a group of rascals: a cutpurse, a swindler, a forger, a bandit, a cult leader, a smuggler, a blackmailer, and two burglars, to teach him their specialties. If the gods would not let him play the part of an industrious, law-abiding bourgeois, at least he would act the rôle they had forced upon him competently.

As it turned out, he did not, on this occasion, need his picklocks, since the door was not locked. Jorian turned the knob, and the door opened with the faintest of squeals.

He well remembered the plan of the penthouse from the days when he had dwelt there. Each night he had one of his five wives sent to him. To allay jealousy, he companied with them in rotation. But the system broke down when one or more became ill or pregnant, and disputes arose over who should take the absent one's place. Finally Jorian settled the argument by saying that he was glad of a night or two off.

Now he found himself in the living room of the apartment. Before him, doors opened to two bedrooms, a bathroom, and the head of a stair leading down to the third story of the palace. In the mild air of an autumnal warm spell, the doors of the bedrooms stood open. One, Jorian supposed, contained Estrildis; the other her lady-in-waiting, whoever she was.

No light burned in these rooms, and little moonlight mitigated the darkness. Jorian wondered how to determine which bedroom harbored which woman. It would not do to awaken the lady-in-waiting by mistake. He must tiptoe to the door of each room, peer in, and, if still in doubt, approach the bed closely enough to settle the question. While he did not know the lady-in-waiting, he hoped at least that she was a brunet, making it easy to distinguish her from the blond Estrildis.

He started toward the left-hand door and at once tripped over an unseen obstacle. He had assumed, without thinking much about the matter, that all the chairs and tables would

13

be in the same places as when he had fled from Xylar. He had forgotten the womanly passion for rearranging the furniture.

The invisible object fell over with an apocalyptic crash. Jorian staggered and recovered, silently cursing a barked shin.

Before Jorian could take a step nearer the left-hand door, a terrific din of barks, growls, and snarls erupted from that bedroom. Jorian had a glimpse of the moonlit, gleaming eyes and bared fangs of some beast bounding toward him.

Swordless, Jorian snatched up the chair he had stumbled over. He brought it up, legs pointing toward the charging watchdog. The animal fetched up against the chair, snapping at the legs, with a force that almost bowled Jorian over. When it fell back to the floor, it tried to circle round Jorian, who turned to keep the chair between himself and the dog.

Women's voices came from the bedrooms: "Who's there?" "Help!" "Who are you?" Then came the buzz of a wheel-lock lighter and a spark of light from the left-hand chamber.

A ghostly figure appeared at the door of the other bedroom. A woman's voice, unfamiliar to Jorian, cried, "Help! Help! Murder!" The woman rushed to the head of the stairway and vanished.

Estrildis, small, stocky, and blond, appeared at the door of the other bedroom, carrying a candle. Still holding off the dog, Jorian shouted: "Darling! It's Jorian! Call this beast off!"

"Oh!" shrieked the little queen. "What—where—come, Thöy! Come back! Come here, Thöy! Good dog! Come, Thöy!"

The dog, which the candlelight revealed as a huge Shvenic mastiff, backed off, growling. Seizing the dog's collar, Estrildis cried: "What do you here, Jorian? I did not expect—"

The cries of the lady-in-waiting came up the stair: "Help! Robbers! Murder! Save the Queen!"

"Sweetheart!" cried Jorian. "I've come to take you away. Come quickly, ere the guards arrive!"

"But how—"

"Never mind! Put down that candle and tie up the dog!"

"But I must know—"

"Damn it, woman, if you don't come instanter—"

A clatter of arms on the stair interrupted Jorian's plea. Men flooded into the living room, the candlelight striking golden gleams from their steel. "Get him!" roared a soldierly voice.

Jorian perceived three naked swords coming toward him, with reinforcements following. He ran out the door to the terrace. There he took three running steps and a flying leap to catch the dangling end of the rope as high up as he could.

"Karadur!" he shouted. "Take us up, fast!"

He began hoisting himself up the rope. The bathtub rose. Before the rope's end had cleared the terrace, a guardsman, putting his sword between his teeth, also caught the rope and began to climb.

The ascent of the tub slowed. On the terrace, other armed figures clustered. One caught the tip of the rope, but the end slipped out of his grasp.

Jorian looked down into the upturned face of the guardsman below him. He thought he recognized the upcurled mustache.

"You're Duvian, are you not?" said Jorian. "I'm Jorian; don't you know me?"

The guardsman, with the sword in his teeth, could only grunt. From below came cries: "Who has a crossbow?" "Well, fetch one, idiot!"

"You'd better let go," said Jorian. "If you are still there when we leave, I'll kick you loose or cut the rope above you. Then you will fall to your death."

The guardsman, holding the rope with his left hand and with his legs clamped around it, took the sword in his right hand and swung it at Jorian's legs, saying: "'Tis my painful duty, O King!"

Jorian kicked, and the sword spun out of the guardsman's grasp. It struck the roof tiles, slid bumpily down the slope of the roof, disappeared over the edge, and landed with a crash on the paving below.

Jorian lowered himself on the rope and aimed another kick, at the guardsman's face. The kick missed, but the soldier relaxed his grip, slid down the rope to the end, and fell a few cubits to the terrace. He landed on one of his comrades, so that the two rolled on the terrace with a clashing of mail. Shouts of furious argument arose from the terrace, now dwindling beneath Jorian as the tub rose.

The jarring snap of a crossbow came up, and a bolt thrummed past. Jorian hoisted himself as fast as he could up to the tub and levered himself over the side. Another crossbow snapped, and a bolt hit the tub, making it ring like a bell. Jorian felt the side of the tub at the place whence the sound had come. His fingers found a bump where the bolt had dented the copper.

"Next thing," he panted, "they'll haul out a catapult. Tell Gorax to get us away with all demonic dispatch!"

"Whither?"

"To Othomae. Tell him to head east. As you said, we do have friends there."

Another crossbow quarrel hummed past below, but the tub was out of range. With the half-moon on their starboard bow, they flew eastward through the night. Jorian was silent, breathing deeply. Then he said:

"A plague, a murrain, and a pox on the Xylarians! By Imbal's brazen balls, I itch to burn their damned city down on their heads. What said your Mulvanian wiseacre about expecting the worst? I had the damnedest run of bad luck; Elidora must have it in for me. 'Twas like one of Physo's comedies. First I tripped over a chair in the dark. Then, Estrildis has somewhere obtained a watchdog the size of a lion, who knew me not. Then—"

"My son," moaned Karadur, "I pray you to reserve the tale till the morrow. I must needs get some sleep betwixt now and dawn. I cannot forgo rest as I could when I was your age."

The wizard curled up in his blanket and was soon snoring. When he calmed down, Jorian found he could smile at himself. He mentally composed a jingle:

16

"A hero who wanted his wife
To carry away without strife,
    Fell over a chair,
    With noise filled the air,
And soon had to flee for his life!"

With nobody to listen to his tale of the abortive rescue,
Jorian soon joined his companion in slumber.

II
THE GRAND DUKE'S PARK

"GORAX INSISTS HE CANNOT PERSEVERE MUCH LONGER," said Karadur, peering into the murk. After leaving Xylar City, they had flown all day and crossed the Othomaean border. The overcast thickened, and rain began to fall. Jorian and Karadur huddled in their cloaks. But the rain fell more and more heavily, soaking them. Water sloshed about the bottom of the tub.

"Have we nought to bail out our ship with?" quavered Karadur. "Gorax complains of the additional weight of the water."

"Now that you mention it," said Jorian, "the tub has an outlet drain with a plug. It should be under that rope."

He inched his way to the faucet end of the tub and pushed aside the coil of rope. The plug was a large cork, driven in so firmly that Jorian's powerful fingers could not dislodge it. He pried the plug out with his dagger, and the bilge water drained out. Night came on.

"I stated that Gorax nears his limit," said Karadur. "He avers that, if not soon permitted to alight, he will collapse and drop us from whatever height we be."

18

"Tell him to slow down," said Jorian. "I know this country well, but I cannot see my hand before my face, let alone landmarks. 'Tis blacker than the inside of a cow. By my reckoning, we should reach Othomae City in two or three hours."

"At least," said Karadur, "we shall not frighten the yokels below to death. As we cannot see them, neither can they perceive us."

Jorian laughed. "Remember that wagoner in Xylar, who leaped from his wain, ran across a field, and burrowed into a haystack to hide?"

"Aye. But your efficient secret service will hear thereof and know we departed to eastward."

"True. But methinks we shall be safe in Othomae. The Othomaeans are ever on bad terms with Xylar. 'Tis one of those silly things where a river changes course, leaving behind a sandbar that belonged to one nation, and now is claimed by another. The dispute had just arisen during my last days as king, so I had no chance to compose it. At any rate, I misdoubt the Othomaeans would extradite us."

"I hope you be right. A lavish bribe oft overrides such parochial passions."

"Then we must needs trust the Xylarian treasurer's parsimony. In my time the post was held by Prithio son of Pellitus, as tight with his golden lions as a Mulvanian tiger with its prey." Jorian peered into the murk, trying to discern some solid object. "Tell Gorax to fly low but slowly, so as not to collide with some tree or steeple. When the moon rises, belike we can find a road or a river to guide us."

Hours later, the rain had slackened to a drizzle. The moon, in its last quarter, gave a faint pearly glow to the clouds overhead. Time ground on.

Peering over the side, Jorian saw plowed fields and now and then a village, a cluster of black rectangles in the darkness. He failed to identify any landmark. Karadur said:

"Gorax avers he be fordone. He warns us to brace ourselves, for he must descend whether we will or no."

There was a feeling of lightness as the tub dropped. The

19

darkness deepened as trees arose about them. With a slight jar, the tub settled on soft ground.

"He bids us farewell," said Karadur. "Know you where we be?"

"Somewhere in Othomae," said Jorian, "unless Gorax have flown us clear across the duchy into Vindium."

Jorian stood up, grunting at the stiffness of his limbs. The rain had ceased, but all around he heard the drip of water from branches.

He hoisted himself out of the tub. The ground seemed a green sward in a small clearing or glade, surrounded by huge trees. Jorian walked around the edges of the glade. Returning, he said:

"I still know not where we are. At least, let us wring the water from our clothes."

Standing in the tub, Jorian removed his garments and wrung them, holding them over the grass. He sneezed. "I hope," he grumbled, "they dry ere we freeze to death.... What's that?"

Something moved about the glade. Its footfalls were practically noiseless; but Jorian could see a darker shadow in the darkness and hear a faint hiss of breathing. Then something sniffed, close to the tub. Two spots of feeble luminosity, barely visible, appeared above the edge of the tub. Jorian recognized an odor.

He was sitting on the coil of rope at the faucet end of the tub. Suddenly he leaped up, waving his arms and uttering an earsplitting scream: *"Ye-ee-ow!"*

There was a spitting snarl and sounds of a body moving swiftly away. "A leopard, I think," said Jorian. "Are you all right, Father Karadur?"

The old wizard was gasping for breath. "Your screech well-nigh arrested my old heart for all eternity."

"Sorry, but I had to surprise the cat to get rid of it. The sky is lightening." Jorian felt his clothes; Karadur's were draped along the opposite side of the tub. "They're not yet dry, but we'd best do them on. The warmth of our bodies will dry them. How about a fire?"

"An excellent idea if feasible. With this all-pervading wet, I have doubts."

Jorian took out his lighter. "Plague! My tinder's wet, and I see not how to get dry tinder. Would your magical fire spell work, think you?"

"If you will fetch fuel, I will essay it."

Soon Jorian had collected fallen branches and twigs. Standing in the tub, Karadur waved his wand, made mystic passes, and uttered words of power. A little blue flame appeared among Jorian's pile of fuel. The flame danced among the branches, now and then evoking a faint hiss; but the fuel would not ignite.

"Alas!" said Karadur. "We can do nought until our wood dries."

Jorian grunted. "I always thought magic was something one resorted to when material means failed; but wizardries seem to fail quite as often."

Karadur sighed. "My son, I fear you have penetrated the secret of secrets, the inmost arcanum."

"Meaning that all you spookers' professions of infinite powers are but a bluff to cozen us laymen?"

"True, alas. We fail as often as do the engineers in the House of Learning in Iraz. But I beseech you, reveal not this dread secret to the vulgus. We wizards have a hard enough time making a living."

Jorian grinned in the darkness. "Since you saved my life, old man, I'll keep your secret." He looked around. The light had grown strong enough to pick out twigs and leaves on trees, although the deciduous trees had lost most of their summer foliage. "By Astis's ivory breasts, what are those?"

To three of the trees surrounding the glade, wooden ladders had been affixed, reaching up until lost in the foliage. Jorian said: "I never heard of trees that grew ladders naturally. They must be the work of men."

"One can imagine erecting such ladders on fruit trees, to facilitate harvesting," said Karadur. "But these are nought but oaks, beeches, and lindens."

"There are beechnuts," said Jorian. "But two of the

21

ladders I see go up oaks. Who would gather unripe acorns?"

"A breeder of swine, belike. But I am not convinced, when it were so much easier to pick them from the ground. Perchance the ladders lead to sentry posts, whence sentinels look out over the land to espy invaders."

"I never heard of aught like that when I served in the Grand Bastard's army," said Jorian. "But what other—oh-oh, Karadur, look behind you!"

The wizard turned and started in alarm. "A unicorn!" he breathed.

The head and forequarters of the animal appeared from out the shrubbery on one side of the glade. The unicorn of Jorian's world was no graceful pseudo-horse. Instead, it was a large member of the rhinoceros tribe, covered with golden-brown hair, with its single horn sprouting from its forehead, above the eyes, instead of its nose.

"If we keep still," whispered Jorian, "maybe he'll go away."

"I fear not," Karadur whispered back. "I detect emanations of rising rage. Methinks we had best prepare to make a dash for one of those ladders."

The unicorn gave an explosive snort, pawed the ground with a triple-hooved foot, and stepped forward.

Jorian murmured: "Soonest begun, soonest done, as said the wise Achaemo. Ready, set, go!"

He vaulted out of the tub and ran for a ladder across the glade from the beast. Karadur followed but, because of his age, fell behind. Jorian waited for him at the foot of the tree, calling: "Faster! Here it comes!"

When the wizard, panting and staggering, reached the tree, Jorian put his large hands around Karadur's waist and boosted the slight oldster several steps up the ladder.

The unicorn made a thunderous charge, snorting like a volcano. It rushed the tub, jerking its head as its horn struck. With a loud *bongg*, the tub flew into the air, scattering the belongings of the two travelers.

"Up! Hasten!" barked Jorian, for the winded Karadur was climbing the ladder with difficulty. Below, Jorian was still in range of the thick, curved horn.

The unicorn lumbered back and forth about the glade,

22

trampling the objects scattered about. It got Jorian's blanket caught on its horn and wheeled about, shaking its head so that the blanket flapped like a flag. When the blanket flew away, the unicorn charged the tub again, tossing it end over end.

Then the animal turned its attention to the travelers on the ladder. It trotted to the oak and tried by rearing up against the trunk to reach Jorian, but he was now beyond range of the horn.

Safely out of reach, Jorian and Karadur continued their climb at a more leisurely pace. When they reached a thick horizontal branch with many smaller boughs for handholds, Jorian climbed out on the branch and sat. Karadur nervously followed. Below, the unicorn cocked its head to keep them in sight.

"Something tells me," said Jorian, "that fellow likes us not. Anyway, I think I know where we are."

"Where?"

"When I served in the Grand Bastard's Foot Guards, there was talk of a plan the Grand Duke cherished. This was to unite his several hunting preserves south of Othomae City into a national park to exhibit wild life. Grand Duke Gwitlac was getting too old and fat to enjoy hunting; and the Grand Bastard Daunas, his half-brother, preferred the pursuit of women to that of deer and boar.

"In either case, they needed money to equip and train their lobster-plated heavy cavalry. So they reckoned that, by stocking the park with beasts both familiar and exotic, they could make a neat income by charging the rabble admission. Visitors would come from other lands to spend their money and thereby be taxed. Our friend below is one of the exotic beasts, since it is native to the northern prairies beyond the Ellornas. Those ladders must have been emplaced for the purpose wherefor we used them, to escape the charge of some beast that misliked gawking visitors."

"All very well," said Karadur. "But how shall we persuade this dratted unicorn to begone?"

Jorian shrugged. "Sooner or later 'twill tire of watching us."

"If we weaken not from starvation and fall out of the tree first," grumbled the seer.

"Well, there was the method whereby King Fusinian escaped the Boar of Chinioc."

Karadur settled himself. "I thought I had heard all your tales of Fusinian the Fox, but this one I know not."

"When Fusinian was King of Kortoli," began Jorian, "he inherited a hunting preserve, like those of this Grand Duke. The preserve was called the Forest of Chinioc. Now, when Fusinian succeeded his father, the incompetent Filoman the Well-meaning, he was kept too busy for several years, what with the war with Aussar and the trouble with the giants called the Teeth of Grimnor, to have time for the Forest of Chinioc.

"After these events, Fusinian settled back to enjoy life, as far as any conscientious ruler can enjoy it despite the harassments of his position. Some of his gentlemen urged him to take up hunting in Chinioc, which, they said, was overrun by wild beasts. In particular, the forest harbored a wild boar of preternatural size, strength, and ferocity. As they described it, it sounded like a buffalo with tusks instead of horns, and the hangers-on filled Fusinian's ears with tales of the glory he would earn by slaying the beast, giving a feast with its flesh, and having its head stuffed and mounted on the palace wall.

"Fusinian did not much care for hunting, but he did like fishing. Moreover, he liked to get off by himself from time to time to mull over the stream of proposals, and bills, and acts, and requests, and treaties, and agreements, and petitions, and memorials constantly urged upon him. For such purposes, the sport of fishing was useful.

"So, one summer day, Fusinian set out with a bodyguard of four troopers and rode to the edge of the Forest of Chinioc. Here he left the troopers, commanding them to remain there unless he should fail to return by an hour before sunset, in which case they should come searching.

"The guards protested, warning the king against the bears, wolves, and leopards in the forest, not to mention

24

the Boar of Chinioc. But Fusinian brushed aside their objections and set out along a trail which, he knew, led to a good trout stream. He bore a pair of fishing rods and a creel containing his luncheon, and he whistled gayly as he plunged into the wold.

"Ere he reached the stream, he heard a grunting, like that engine in the House of Learning in Iraz, whereby one of the servants hopes to get useful work by the power of steam. And then the Boar of Chinioc ambled out from between the trees. At the sight of Fusinian, the animal grunted, pawed the earth, and lowered its head to charge.

"The beast was not quite the size of a buffalo, but it was certainly large enough. The bristles on its back came up to the height of Fusinian's chin; and Fusinian had no arms save a knife for cleaning fish.

"As the monster bounded forward, the king dropped his fishing rods and sprang for the nearest tree, a big beech like that one yonder. Although a small man, he was wiry and active, and he scrambled up into the branches. Below, the boar reared up against the trunk; but it could not reach Fusinian, now perched on a branch as we are.

"Fusinian thought that, if he sat long enough, the boar would lose interest and go away. But hours passed, and the boar stubbornly remained below. Every time Fusinian moved, the boar circled about, looking up and grunting ferociously.

"Fusinian began to worry about his guards and his wife and his kingdom, and he decided that he must escape in one way or another. He tried shouting, hoping his guards would hear; but they were too far away.

"He thought of other expedients, such as whittling a branch into a pole and tying his knife to it to make a spear. He actually cut one branch of about the right size for the purpose, but found it too limber. It would simply bend and break ere it drove a blade through the boar's thick hide.

"Next, he thought to make a diversion. He did off his hat, jerkin, and hose and constructed a dummy, using his fishhooks to pin these garments together and leafy branches

25

for stuffing. Then he crept out along a branch and hung the dummy by means of his spare fishing line at such a height that the boar could not quite reach it.

"Creeping back, he shook the branch so that the dummy bobbed up and down and swayed from side to side. The boar, seeing what looked like Fusinian dancing in the air above it, went into a paroxysm of rage, snorting like a thunderstorm and leaping about beneath the dummy, striving to reach and slash it.

"Meanwhile Fusinian climbed down the tree on the side away from the boar and ran for his life. When he could no longer hear the thrashing and grunting of the boar, he stopped with the realization that he was lost.

"Steering by the sun, he headed back toward the edge of the Forest of Chinioc. In mid-afternoon, he came to a fence that marked the boundary. Continuing on, he found himself in cultivated fields; but he realized that he must be a long way from where he had entered the forest. The first person he saw was a farmer hoeing weeds. Approaching, he said: 'God den, goodman. May I—'

"At that, the farmer turned to shout toward his house: 'Inogen! Run to fetch the constable! 'Tis a madman we have, running about the land naked!' For, indeed, Fusinian was naked but for his boots, underwear not having been in use in his time. Meanwhile the farmer ported his hoe like a weapon, in case Fusinian should come closer.

"'My good man,' quoth Fusinian, 'you are mistaken—a natural error, belike, but a mistake natheless. Know that I am King Fusinian, your sovran lord. If you will be so kind as to lend me some garments—' Whereupon the rustic shouted louder than before: 'Inogen! Hasten! The madman is proclaiming himself king!'

"The farmer's wife ran out of the house, mounted a mule, and set out at a gallop. Fusinian tried to explain how he had fallen into this curious plight; but the more he talked, the more alarmed the rustic became, threatening Fusinian with his hoe until the king had to leap back to avoid being struck.

"Then came a clatter of hooves, and the farmer's wife reappeared on her mule, accompanied by a constable on horseback. The latter swung down with a jingle of mail and approached the king, saying: 'Easy, now, easy, fellow! Come with me to the lazarette, where our learned physicians will cure you. Come along, poor fellow!'

"The constable approached Fusinian and made a snatch at him, but the king leaped back and ran. The constable ran after, clanking and jingling, and so did the farmer. The farmer's two sons, just returning from school, joined the chase. So did other yokels. Soon Fusinian found himself pursued by a score of men and boys, some armed and all shouting: 'Seize the madman, ere he slay someone in his frenzy!'

"A swift runner, Fusinian long kept ahead of the pursuit. But, as one pursuer became winded and dropped back, another joined the chase, so that in time the little king faltered. Then men on horseback galloped up on either side of him, one being the constable whom the farmer's wife had summoned. So Fusinian stopped, holding up his hands to show he was harmless. Between gasps, he tried once more to explain, but none heeded his words.

"Instead, someone knotted a rope around his neck and gave the other end to the constable, who said: 'Now, poor fellow, ye shall come along whether ye will or no.' The constable turned his horse away and tugged on the rope, so that Fusinian was forced to trot along. And thus, at sunset, they came to the nearest village, called Dimilis.

"They fetched the magistrate, who arrived at the jailhouse much put out by having to leave his dinner half-eaten. When he had heard the stories of the first farmer and the constable, he asked Fusinian: 'And what have ye to say, my featherless fowl?'

"Fusinian said: 'Your Honor, it is true that I am King Fusinian.'

"'Hah!' said the magistrate. "A likely story! Where are your crown, your robes of state, your train of attendants? Forsooth, we have here not merely insanity but also high treason. Clap this knave in irons!'

"'Your Honor!' quoth Fusinian. 'To prove my veracity, I can recite the coronation oath. I can list the ancestors of the royal line for fifteen generations. Fetch someone who knows me! Send word to the court!' But no heed did anyone pay.

"None knows how much further this farce would have gone, but just then two of Fusinian's guardsmen appeared, demanding news of their King. When they saw Fusinian, laden with chains, being led off to a cell, they dropped to one knee, crying: 'Your Majesty! What scoundrels have entreated you thus? Command us to slay them!'

"A great silence fell amongst the folk gathered in the jailhouse. Each tried to look as if he had just happened by on other business and knew nought of the dispute over the naked man's identity. Each tried to hide behind his fellows, and some of those near the door tiptoed out and ran for it, until one of the guardsmen blocked the door.

"Fusinian smiled through the dirt wherewith he was covered, saying: 'Hail, Baldolf and Cumber! Am I glad to see you! How came you so opportunely?'

"A guardsman spoke: 'Your Majesty, when the sun stood a hand's breadth from the horizon, we followed your trail into the forest. Soon we saw what we thought was Your Majesty hanged from a branch of a tree, which gave us a frightful shock; but we found this was merely Your Majesty's garments stuffed with brush. Although we could not imagine the reason for this, we agreed that two of us should continue to search the forest, whilst the other two hastened to Dimilis and spread the alarum for our King's disappearance.'

"'I will explain,' said Fusinian, but at that moment the magistrate and all the other local folk fell on their knees and groveled, crying: 'Mercy, Great King! We meant no harm! We thought but to do our duty! We have wives and children! Mercy, we beseech thee!'

"'Get up!' said Fusinian sharply. 'To say I am pleased by today's events were stretching the truth; but I do not massacre my subjects, however idiotically they comport themselves. Magistrate Colgrin! For your haste in passing judgment ere the evidence be in, I will levy a small fine upon you. You shall remove your jacket and trews and give them to me, instanter!'

"So pleased was the magistrate to get away with his

life that he stripped off the garments and handed them over forthwith, leaving himself naked but for his shoes and chain of office. Fusinian donned the garments, which fitted him ill since Colgrin was fat. With his two guards, the king strode out of the jailhouse, mounted his horse—which the guards had led with them—and galloped away. But thereafter Fusinian was more cautious about leaving his guards and going off by himself."

Karadur said: "An edifying tale, showing how our perceptions of rank and authority are swayed by superficial things. But our unicorn shows no disposition to depart, and I misdoubt we could distract it as your king did with the boar."

Jorian put a finger to his lips, whispering: "I hear voices." The voices waxed, and a swishing of branches told of the movement of a large body. The unicorn looked across the glade and snorted.

Out from the trees lumbered an elephant, a huge Mulvanian tusker with people on its back. As the animal came closer, Jorian saw that a broad plank was secured lengthwise along its spine. Eight people sat on this plank in two rows, back to back, with their feet resting on footboards along the elephant's sides. A turbaned Mulvanian sat astride the elephant's neck and guided the beast.

One rider was a man in an unfamiliar uniform, who was lecturing the seven others on the plank. In a stentorian voice, this man said: "There you see a unicorn from the steppes of Shven. Its scientific name is *Elasmotherium*, and the philosophers tell us it is related to the rhinoceros of Beraoti. Although a grass-eater, it is short-tempered and dangerous if approached on foot...."

The unicorn turned and trotted away from the glade. Jorian quickly lost sight of it. A young elephant-rider called out: "Master Ranger, what's that red thing yonder?" The child pointed to the battered bathtub.

The ranger spoke to the mahout, who guided the elephant toward the tub and the debris of Jorian's and Karadur's belongings. The ranger said: "By Zevatas's brazen beard, what's this? It looks as if some vagabonds had

29

camped here and departed leaving their litter. There is punishment for littering. But what's this object? It looks like a large bathtub, but how could such a thing get here?"

The child spoke again: "Master Ranger, there are your vagabonds, sitting in that big tree!"

"Oho!" said the ranger. He spoke to the mahout, who brought the elephant to stand beneath the branches of Jorian's tree. "Fry my guts, but here we have a brace of poachers, caught red-handed! But the game they flushed proved larger than they expected."

"Excuse me, sir," said Jorian, "but you are misinformed. We are not poachers, merely a pair of travelers dropped into your park by happenstance."

"A likely story!" The ranger turned to his sightseers. "Now you shall behold how we of the Ranger Corps dispose of such knaves." He raised a bugle to his mouth and blew a call. The call was answered from afar.

"How got you in?" the ranger asked. "You did not come in the gate and sign the register, or you would not be wandering the park unescorted. Your presence alone proves your guilt."

Jorian pointed to the bathtub, lying across the glade. "We came in yonder tub, upheld by sorcery. When our demon became exhausted, he dropped us into this glade. Since it was at night, we knew not where we were."

"Ha!" said the ranger. "Try to convince the judge of that!"

"Good my sir," persisted Jorian, "we are quite respectable folk, despite appearances. I have served in the Grand Bastard's Foot Guards and studied at the Academy. If you will ask Doctor Gwiderius—"

"You waste your breath, poacher," said the ranger. "If you shut not your gob, 'twill be the worse for you."

After a further wait, three rangers on horses cantered out from between the trees. After talk between them and the one on the elephant, the latter spoke to his mahout, and the elephant started off into the forest. Jorian could hear the ranger's voice, fading with distance:

"...the unicorn is an animal of solitary habits, keeping

company with another of its kind only at the mating season...."

Of the three newly arrived rangers, two bore crossbows. The third, who appeared to be in command, said: "Come down now, poachers. But think not to run off through the woods, unless you crave a bolt in the brisket."

"May we gather our belongings, pray?" said Jorian, reaching the ground.

"Aye, but be quick about it!"

Half an hour later, Jorian and Karadur arrived at the park entrance. Some of their belongings, such as Jorian's set of small cooking utensils, had been smashed beyond repair. The rest were rolled up in blankets, which they bore on their backs like refugees.

Another elephant was being prepared for a sightseeing trip. It lay on its belly, and the next batch of sightseers was climbing a ladder placed against its side to take their places on its back. Several more of the animals were tethered to stakes in a row, rhythmically swaying and stuffing greenery into their mouths.

The two travelers were surrounded by rangers, disarmed, and hustled into a small detention room. "Here you shall wait, poachers," a ranger said, "until Ranger Ferrex returns from his tour."

The door was slammed and bolted on the outside. A bench was the only furniture; the only light came from a little window high up, about a handspan square.

"Now I know how your King Fusinian felt when none would listen to his rational explanation," said Karadur. "Could you open the door with your picklocks?"

"If it were closed by a proper lock, yea; but my little teasers were useless against bolts."

During the wait, Jorian relieved his boredom by composing a poem on their latest misadventure. The first stanza ran:

"Two gallant adventurers, hardy and bold,
        To Othomae endeavored to fly;

31

But their demon gave out o'er the Grand Ducal wold,
  So now in the lockup they cry!"

Jorian had reached the fifth stanza when the door opened. Ranger Ferrex beckoned. "Come, poachers!"

They were handcuffed together, taken to a wagon with seats, and loaded aboard with their gear. Ranger Ferrex got in and sat facing them. The driver whipped up the horses. The wagon rattled over the dirt road for an hour, passing fields and villages, until Othomae City appeared on the horizon.

On the way, Jorian and Karadur conversed in Mulvanian. This made Ferrex scowl, but he did not try to stop them. They agreed that Jorian might as well give his true name, since he wanted to get in touch with people he knew.

At the jailhouse, the ranger told his story to the magistrate, Judge Flollo, and Jorian repeated the tale he had told the ranger. The magistrate said:

"I cannot let you out on bail, since as foreigners you have no local ties to assure your appearance for trial. You profess to have used sorcery to come hither; but if you be sorcerers, you could summon another demon or work a spell with your sorcerous implements and escape."

"But Your Honor!" protested Jorian. "If we be sorcerers, then our tale is proven true. Hence we cannot be poachers."

"Nought hinders a sorcerer from trying his hand at poaching, if that be his bent." The magistrate hefted Jorian's purse and poured out its load of coins. "A veritable fortune! Whence got you this money? Have you robbed a royal treasury?"

"Not robbed, Your Honor. It's a long story. As you see, the coins are of the Kingdom of Penembei, where I was employed to repair the clocks in the tower—"

"Never mind. The money shall be sequestered and returned to you, minus the cost of your prison victuals, when and if you are acquitted of the charge of poaching."

"But, Your Honor, if I be so well provided, I had no

need to sit out in the rain all night in hope of snaring a hare. Let me tell you how—"

"I cannot take time to hear your tale, prisoner; I have many more cases to decide. Your presence unescorted in the park is *prima facie* evidence of wrongdoing; so whether your story be true or false will be for the trial judge to decide. Take them away, bailiff."

"Come, you two," said a heavyset, scar-faced man in a shabby black uniform. Jorian and Karadur were led down a corridor to another cell. This, Jorian found, had a single, heavily barred window, high up. As the bailiff closed the door, he said: "Did I hear you give your name as Jorian of Ardamai?"

"Aye. What about it?"

"Do ye not recall a fellow soldier named Malgo?"

"Yea, now that you mention it." Jorian looked sharply at the bailiff. "By Imbal's iron yard, methinks I see my old comrade-in-arms!"

"Comrade, hell!" snorted Malgo. "Ye be the bastard who gave me a beating. And now I have you where I want you! Ye'll be sorry ye ever laid a finger on me!"

"But that was seven years ago—" began Jorian. Malgo walked heavily away, paying no attention.

"What was all that?" asked Karadur.

"When Malgo and I were recruits in the Grand Bastard's army, Malgo was the company bully. He made life especially hard for one lad who, whatever he was good for, was not cut out for a soldier. He was a spindly little whelp and awkward, forever stepping off on the wrong foot or dropping his pike. So Malgo took delight in tormenting him.

"One day I found the lad backed into a corner, while Malgo poked, pinched, and otherwise mistreated him, all the while telling him how worthless he was. I suspected that Malgo had made certain demands of the youth and had been denied. Thinking it time for Malgo to receive a dose of his own physic, I hauled him round and gave him a drubbing. I got a bloody nose and a black eye, but you should have seen him!"

"All very gallant," said Karadur, "but it redounds not to our advantage now. Would we had used one of your pseudonyms, such as—what did you call yourself when you first fled hither from Xylar?"

"Nikko of Kortoli. You may be right, but it's too late now."

During the following days, Bailiff Malgo, while careful to keep out of Jorian's reach, found ingenious ways to torment the prisoners. He made sure that their food ration was but half that of the other prisoners, and consisted of the least edible parts of the day's serving. The food was delivered by Malgo's assistant, a huge, half-witted youth with a vacant smile.

When Jorian demanded to see the magistrate to complain, Malgo said he would carry the message. Soon he came back, saying that the magistrate refused. Jorian suspected that the message had never been delivered.

When Jorian asked for water, Malgo fetched a cup, then poured it on the floor outside the cell, laughing.

Jorian asked for writing materials, to send a note to Doctor Gwiderius and another to the wizardess Goania. Malgo furnished paper and pen. When Jorian had written the notes and handed them through the bars, Malgo tore them up, laughing.

Malgo refused to let his helper take out and empty the commode, so that the cell came to stink. The stench attracted swarms of flies. Malgo sometimes stood in the hall outside, laughing at the prisoners' efforts to slap the pests. "Let's hope this lasts not till next summer's heat," grumbled Jorian.

At last Jorian said: "Holy Father, can't you work up a spell to get us out of here?"

"Nay, my son. The little spells I could perform without my paraphernalia would accomplish nought. Besides, I sense that a contraspell has already been laid about this edifice, so that none of my spells would succeed. How about your picklocks? The locks on these cells, meseems, are of the sort for which they are suited."

"Aye, but my little ticklers are in my wallet, which is in the magistrate's custody."

"He also has my magical accessories in his charge."

"This is ridiculous!" growled Jorian. "Here we are, two harmless travelers with local friends of influence and repute, locked up through a series of mischances, and we cannot even communicate with anyone who could help us!"

"If we shouted our message through yonder window, belike we could persuade someone to carry a message."

Jorian clapped a hand to his forehead. "Why didn't I think of this sooner? I'm a stupid clod. We've wasted a quarter-moon in this stinking cell. If I stand on one of the stools...."

The stool brought Jorian's face up to the window. He found himself looking down from the second story of the jailhouse on to the street below.

"Methinks we're on Amaethius Street," he told Karadur. "There are a few passersby. Ho there, young man! You with the red cap! Wouldst earn a golden royal of Penembei by bearing a message?"

The boy hurried on. Jorian tried again and again with other pedestrians. At last he gave up. "They must be so used to hearing cries from prisoners that they heed them not."

A raucous laugh came from beyond the bars. Malgo stood there, saying: "Waste your breath if ye will, noble Jorian! Know that there's a law against carrying messages for prisoners, and we keep an officer posted to see that none flouts the rule."

Jorian got down. When Malgo went away, Jorian said: "Still, there must be something." He sat frowning in thought and said at last: "Some have said that I have not a bad singing voice, albeit untrained. If I gave the folk below a little concert, at a regular hour each day, perchance I could draw a crowd who would gather to hear. Sooner or later the word would get out, and one of our friends would hear of it."

"I cannot see how it would hurt to try," said Karadur.

Jorian hoisted himself back on the stool and, in his powerful bass, began singing one of his jingles, to a tune

35

from an operetta by Galliben and Silfero. The first stanza ran:

> "Oh, some like the steaming jungle hot,
> Where serpents swarm and the sun shines not,
> And sweat runs off and your garments rot;
> But I prefer a more temperate spot—
> Novaria, my Novaria."

By the end of the third stanza, a cluster of pedestrians had coagulated in the street below, staring up. Malgo appeared outside the bars, roaring: "Stop that hellish noise!"

Jorian grinned over his shoulder at the bailiff and continued on through the six stanzas he had previously composed. He added a new one:

> "Some take to the ice-clad arctic waste,
> Where man by the snow bear fierce is faced,
> Or else by ravenous wolves is chased;
> But as for me, I'd return in haste
> To Novaria, good Novaria."

Malgo continued to bawl objections, but he did not enter the cell. Jorian added several other songs, then stepped down. "It's a start," he said.

He spent the rest of the day and much of the night remembering the verses he had casually tossed off over the years and trying to match them to tunes he remembered. The following afternoon, at about the same time, he delivered another recital. Malgo shouted: "For this, I'll see to it ye never go free! Ye shall rot here for ay!"

Jorian ignored the threat and continued his singing. On the sixth day after the first recital, the half-wit appeared at the bars with keys. To Jorian's astonishment, the youth unlocked the cell door, saying: "Ye come, now."

They found Magistrate Flollo talking with Doctor Gwiderius. The professor beamed through his bushy gray beard. "Jorian! My onetime pupil! When I heard those songs with the quadruple-alpha rhyme scheme, I suspected 'twas you, since that was your favorite form despite its difficulties. You are free, and there are your effects. Who is your companion?"

Jorian introduced Karadur, adding: "What—how—"

"I shall tell you later. Have you a place to stay? I cannot lodge you in my own house, because we have visiting kinfolk."

Jorian shrugged. "I suppose I'll stay at Rhuys's inn, the Silver Dragon, as I did before." He turned to the magistrate. "Sir, where is Master Malgo?"

"Oh, when Doctor Gwiderius brought the order for your release, the bailiff was seized by sudden pains internal. Avouching that he suffered an affliction of the bowels, he begged the rest of the day off. So I let him go. Why, Master Jorian?"

Jorian looked at the knuckles of his fist. "Oh, I just thought I should like to bid him a fond farewell." He turned to Gwiderius. "Where's the public bathhouse?"

✠✠✠✠✠✠✠✠✠✠✠✠✠✠✠✠✠

III

THE INN
OF THE
SILVER DRAGON

JORIAN SAID: "GOOD MASTER RHUYS, I, TOO, AM GLAD TO SEE
you again. I trust the dinner will make a pleasant contrast
to those I've enjoyed as a guest of the Grand Duchy."

"I heard of your trouble with the park rangers," said
Rhuys. The proprietor of the Silver Dragon was a small,
seedy-looking man with thinning, graying hair and pouched
eyes.

Jorian, Karadur, and Doctor Gwiderius occupied a table
in Rhuys's common room, drinking wine and telling tales
while awaiting their repast. Jorian had sent one of Rhuys's
pot boys with a message to the wizardess Goania, whom
he had met on his previous visit to Othomae. He said to
Gwiderius:

"But Doctor, you haven't explained how you got me
out so featly."

The learned man chuckled. "I have a cousin named
Rodaus, a usurer by trade. This cousin owed me a favor
for giving his mediocrity of a son a passing grade in one
of my courses at the Academy. The Grand Bastard seeks

38

a loan from Rodaus, and they have disputed the rate of interest."

"To finance his armored horse, belike?" said Jorian. In Othomae, the Grand Duke ran civil affairs, while the Grand Bastard, the eldest illegitimate son of the previous Grand Duke, commanded the army.

"No doubt. Anyway, I passed the word to Rodaus, assuring him that, knowing you from yore, I was sure your release were no injustice. So Rodaus, in return for a promise to drop all charges, let the noble Daunus have his loan for half a percentum point less than he had demanded."

Nodding toward Karadur, Jorian smiled. "My dear old preceptor insists that all decisions be made on a basis of abstract, impersonal right and wrong. But I note that in sore straits, he lets expediency rule his course, even as we common clods." He counted the money in his purse. "By Imbal's brazen arse, they forgot to deduct the cost of my food in jail!"

"They forgot not," said Gwiderius. " 'Twas part of the bargain."

Jorian was volubly thanking the savant when the door opened, and in came the wizardess Goania, a tall, middle-aged woman with graying hair. After her came her bodyguard, a big, gross, porcine man. Following him, a tall, black-haired young woman in a grass-green gown came in. She was not beautiful, but striking-looking, with the lines of a hard life graven on her irregular features. She bore a black eye.

Jorian rose. "Hail, Mistress Goania!" he called. "Ah there, Boso and Vanora! How wag your worlds?"

The stout man growled something in a surly tone. The young woman cried: "Jorian! How good to see you again!" She hurried over to embrace Jorian, who showed no great eagerness to respond. Two years before, just after his escape from Xylar, he had engaged in a brief and stormy love affair with Vanora, who then became the companion of the piggy-eyed Boso son of Triis. She and Boso sat down by themselves at a small table across the common room.

"Now, Jorian," said Goania Aristor's daughter, in the tone of an aunt setting a wayward nephew to rights, "sit down and tell all. What's this wild tale of your rolling into the ducal park in a tub on wheels, and there slaying the Grand Duke's prize unicorn?"

Jorian laughed. "It wasn't like that, albeit what truly befell us was quite as strange." He plunged into the story of his escape from Iraz in the demon-borne tub, his failure to abduct Estrildis, and his unwitting landing in the park. When he told of his imprisonment, Gwiderius said:

"I am shocked, Jorian! Prison management was supposed to have been reformed; I was on the committee to make recommendations to the Grand Duke. But I see things have slipped back into their usual rut. True, persons like this bailiff are not always of highest character, but we cannot permit such persecution of one who is not even tried! I shall get word of this to His Grace."

Jorian thought a moment and said: "Thanks, but you had better let the matter lie, Doctor. If I meet Malgo alone, I may take him on at fisticuffs; but meanwhile the less I'm involved with the ducal court the better. Someone might get the idea of selling me to the Xylarian Regency for enough to equip another squadron of lancers."

Rhuys served their dinners. Later, Jorian said: "Let's talk of how I shall get my darling Estrildis out of her gilded cage. I cannot raise an army to besiege the city, and our flying bathtub is out of service. What else can be had in flying spells?"

"Well," said Karadur, "there is Sir Fendix's flying broom, and Antonerius's tame wyvern, and Coel's spell, whereby he changes himself into a vulture. But all have shortcomings. Fendix has twice been nearly slain when his broom went out of control; it is subject to something he terms a 'tailspin.' The wyvern is but half domesticated and may yet devour Antonerius at one gulp. And Coel is said to have sold his soul into a thousand years' bondage on the Third Plane in return for his shape-changing power. Nay, I see no good prospect for another aerial assault. Besides, the Xylarians will have posted guards on the roof."

"Then we should need more than just me," said Jorian. "I wonder—"

Goania spoke up: "Meseems the Xylarians, fearing another raid from the air, would have moved your queen to some less-exposed place."

Jorian grunted. "You make sense as usual, my dear aunt. How shall we find out?"

"Leave it to me," said the wizardess. "Is this tabletop clean? Good. I shall probe the Xylarian palace. You!" she spoke to a pot boy. "Fetch me a clean towel, pray."

With the towel she wiped the inside of her empty wine glass. Then she dropped a pinch of green powder into the glass. She muttered an incantation, whereupon the powder smoldered and sent up a thread of purple smoke.

"Break not one of Rhuys's best glasses!" said Jorian.

"Hush, boy!" She leaned over the glass and inhaled. For some moments she sat with her eyes closed. Then she muttered:

"It is dark...nay, there is a light, a yellow light...the light of an oil lamp....I am in an underground chamber...there is a door with iron bars. The walls are of rough stone, as in a cell or dungeon...but there are hangings on the walls and a carpet on the floor, as if the place had been made more comfortable...I see a small, blond woman, seated at what appears to be a dressing table...she seems to be sewing. The scene blurs, as if some force were pushing my second sight away. All over!"

She took deep breaths and opened her eyes. Jorian said: "Me-thinks I know where she is, in the largest cell of our dungeon. But how shall I gain access thereto?"

"Has the palace no secret tunnels?" asked Gwiderius. "Palaces and castles ofttimes possess them, to let the chief man escape if the stronghold falls to a foe."

"Nay," said Jorian. "I investigated when I was king, since such an exit would have let me flee their beheading ceremony. But though I prowled the lower parts of the palace, tapped the walls, and consulted the oldest plans of the edifice, no trace of an escape tunnel could I find. It had been futile to ask the Xylarians to dig me one, since their efforts were devoted to thwarting my escape."

"Could one dig such a tunnel from the outside and bore through the cell wall with miner's tools?" asked Goania.

"Conceivable but not likely. One would have either to

start outside the city, or take a house inside and bore down through the floor and then on a level until one reached the palace. Such a task would take months, and I doubt if I could remain undetected so long. For example, one would have to dispose of the dirt dug from the tunnel without arousing suspicion. Since Xylar City is built on soft, alluvial soil, one must bring in timber to line one's tunnel and shore it up, lest it collapse on one.

"Then how could one be sure of reaching the right underground chamber? With but a slight error in deduced reckoning, one might break into the armory or the treasury instead of Estrildis's chamber. And wherever one broke in, it would be a noisy process, which would alert the guards.

"Finally, unless the Xylarian spy system have deteriorated since my day, any such doings would soon come to the ears of the Regency Council. And then...." Jorian brought the edge of his hand sharply against his neck.

"What then?" said Karadur.

"Since the Xylarians have blocked the avenues to direct assault, I suppose we must resort to magic. What can our professionals of the occult offer?"

Goania and Karadur exchanged glances. The wizardess said: "Alas, I am more a seer than a thaumaturge or sorcerer. I have no means of getting your lass out of an underground cell."

"Couldn't you," Jorian asked Karadur, "somehow recall Gorax from the Fifth Plane?"

"Nay, my son. My sorcerous powers are straitly limited. I obtained control of Gorax through a colleague, Doctor Valdonius, whom you remember from Tarxia. I saved him from a magical predicament, and in gratitude he transferred Gorax, whom he had evoked, to me and imprisoned the demon in this ring."

"How about other demons?"

Karadur shrugged. "Nay; 'tis not my specialty."

Jorian growled: "My two great magical experts seem to have proven a rope of sand. Know you one whom you would trust for such an operation?"

Gwiderius spoke: "One of my fellow pedants at the Academy, Doctor Abacarus, might help."

"What is his line of work?"

"He is professor of occult philosophy, and I believe he performs sorcerous experiments on the side. If you wish, I will present you to him."

"I do wish, thank you," said Jorian. "The sooner the better."

Karadur yawned. "Forgive me, gentles, for interrupting this congenial evening; but an old man wearies fast. I shall withdraw, leaving the rest to enjoy—"

"Karadur!" said Goania. "You shan't remain here tonight. I would fain discuss a new method of astral projection with you; so you shall pass the night at my house."

Jorian spoke up: "Well, Mistress Goania, if you are taking Doctor Karadur—"

"I cannot also accommodate you, young sir," she said sharply. "For one, there is not enough room; for two, the doctor threatens not my repute, whereas a lusty, young springald like you indubitably would. Come along, Karadur. Come, Boso and Vanora. Good night all!"

She swept out, followed by the others. Gwiderius soon excused himself also.

Jorian had just gotten his boots off when there came a knock. "Who is it?" he asked.

"I, Vanora. Pray let me in!"

Jorian unbarred the door. She entered, saying: "Oh, Jorian, how good it is to see you again! What a fool I was not to have kept my grip on you when I had you!"

"Whence got you that black eye?" asked Jorian.

"Boso gave it. We had a dispute this morn."

"The bastard! Do you want me to give him one?"

"Nay. So long as I'm his leman, I must betimes endure his fist."

"What caused it?"

"Forsooth, 'twas not wholly his fault, for I had sorely provoked the lout."

Having received some of Vanora's provocations in the

past, Jorian understood this. He even felt a twinge of sympathy for Boso. "How did you get away?"

"Oh, Boso's asleep, and my mistress and your Mulvanian spooker are so deep in magical converse that they never noticed as I slipped out." She put on the pleading look that Jorian had seen before. "Know you what night this is?"

Jorian frowned. "It is the last day of the Bear, is it not?"

"Aye. But does it mean aught to you?"

Jorian looked puzzled. "Nought special. Should it?"

"It was just two years ago that we parted in Othomae, when I took up with that brute Boso."

"So it is; but what of that?"

She moved closer. "Wilt not let a poor drabby correct her error?" She grasped Jorian's hand and drew it inside her gown, so that he grasped her right breast, while looking up at him with slightly parted lips.

Jorian felt a familiar stirring in his tissues. But he said: "My dear Vanora, that is over and done with." Although his pulse quickened, he withdrew his hand. "I'll have no more of those games until I get my own wife back."

"Now, forsooth! Since when have you become a holy anchorite? You were lusty enough two years ago, and at your age you cannot blame senility. Sit down!"

She gave him a sudden push, so that he sat down on the edge of the bed. She undid a clasp, dropped the emerald-green gown around her feet, sat down in Jorian's lap, and began to kiss and fondle him, murmuring: "Then you were the most satisfying of all my lovers, stiff as a sword blade and hardy as Mount Aravia. Oh, my true love, take me back! For two years I have yearned for the feel of your love, penetrating—"

"Get off!" he said sharply. In another moment, he knew, he would cast good resolutions to the winds, although he knew that Vanora would bring him nothing but trouble. As Goania had told him once, Vanora had the unfortunate talent of not only being chronically unhappy herself but of making those around her unhappy as well. "If you get not to your feet, I'll stand up and dump you on the floor!"

Pouting, she stood up but remained swaying nakedly

44

before him. "What has changed, Jorian? Are you having one of your sudden attacks of virtue? You know it will pass."

Jorian looked up at her, secretly happy that he had not been compelled to stand up. This would, under the circumstances, have been difficult. "Nay; I merely resolved to do what I promised myself. Call it exercising my strength of character, if you wish; like lifting weights to enlarge one's thews."

"Why all that pain and trouble? Since the wizard Aello discovered a really effective contraceptive spell, nobody—well, hardy anybody—heeds all those old rules about who may bed whom any more."

"A philosopher at the Academy told me that our present promiscuity is but a fad that comes and goes, like fashions in hats or cloaks. Anyway, I remember you as careless with your contraceptive spells."

"Well, I've never gotten pregnant yet. Of course, were you the father, I might not mind...."

Jorian was of several minds: to lay her on the bed and have at her; to push her out of the room and throw her dress after her.... Each course had its perils. If he treated her roughly, she might make trouble between him and Goania; he did not underestimate her capacity for stirring up quarrels. Or she might incite Boso to assault him. While he did not fear Boso, he did not want either complication, for such hostilities would interrupt his quest for Estrildis.

He fumbled for an excuse that would send her away disappointed perhaps, but not bent on revenge. At last his storytelling talent rescued him. He said:

"Sit on yonder chair, my dear, and I'll tell you what has changed. You remember my adventure on Rennum Kezymar, when I saved those twelve slave girls from the retired executioners of Ax Castle?"

"Aye. That was a noble deed, worthy of my Jorian."

"Thank you; but I have not told you half the story. As the *Talaris* sailed toward Janareth, the girls were naturally grateful at not being used to demonstrate those fellows' skills at flaying, blinding, beheading, and other quaint specialties of the executioner's art. The first night out from

45

the island, one of the girls—I think her name was Wenna—
came to my berth to show her gratitude, and I did not deny
her.

"Next day, about noon, this Wenna was seized by horrible pains and convulsions. Within an hour, for all that
Doctor Karadur could do, she was dead. We buried the
poor little thing at sea.

"The following night, another girl came to me, and
again I sought to pleasure her. And again, the following
day, she was seized by cramps and convulsions and died.
We wept as her body was committed to the deep.

"These sad events aroused a lively suspicion that there
was a connection betwixt their carnal congress with me
and their untimely fates. So Doctor Karadur performed a
great conjuration. When he came out of his trance, he had
located the source of the trouble. The executioners, such
as were left after their free-for-all battle, were naturally
incensed when they found I had carried off the slaves wher-
eon they meant to monstrate their skills at the banquet.
The wife of one, Karadur discovered, was a witch. At her
husband's behest, she put a curse upon me, so that any
dame with whom I copulated would die within twelve
hours.

"Now, Vanora dear, if you wish to take a chance that
the curse have lost its potency, let's have at it. But say
not that I failed to warn you!"

She looked at him slantwise. "That flapping tongue of
yours was always fertile in expedients," she said. "I know
not whether to believe you. At Metouro you were ready
enough."

"I was a little drunk and had forgotten the curse. Besides, your beauty had driven all other thoughts out of my
head."

"Hm; I see you're still as smooth-tongued a flatterer as
any courtier. Well, how about Estrildis? If the curse be
true, her demise will soon follow your reunion."

"Oh, I won't touch Estrildis, even if I can get her out
of Xylar, until the curse be lifted. Karadur is sure that he
and Goania can devise an effective counterspell."

"I still think you're lying your head off."

"There's an easy way to find out," said Jorian, standing up and unlacing his shirt. "If that is what you want...." He pulled off his breeches.

"I see that not all of you has turned ascetic," she said.

"Who said it had? If you're fain to take a chance, lie down and spread out."

She hesitated, then stooped and picked up her dress. "Nay, you're as hard to grasp as a greased eel. What befell the remaining girls?"

"I sent them home from Janareth. Well, wilt chance it nor not? I cannot maintain this stance all night."

With a sigh she slipped on her dress. "Nay, I will not. I had but thought.... But never mind. Boso may be a brute, but all his members are in working order, without curses save that of stupidity. Good night!"

Jorian watched her go with a wry smile and a mixture of relief and regret. It took all his strength not to call her back and confess that the story was a lie. Actually, he had not carnally known any of the twelve slave girls until the night before they parted in Trimandilam. Then Mnevis, the leader, had insinuated herself into his bed without encouragement from him.

He had not told Vanora of his passing off Mnevis and the others at the court of Trimandilam as the Queen of Algarth and her ladies-in-waiting. He was already on the Mulvanians' grudge list for his theft of the Kist of Avlen. He did not wish to give Vanora information that she might, in a fit of malevolence, use against him. Naturally a frank, open, cheerful soul, with a tendency to talk too much and indiscreetly, he was learning caution the hard way.

Doctor Abacarus proved a bald, fat, clean-shaven, red-faced man with a high voice. He reminded Jorian of the eunuchs he had encountered in Iraz; but Gwiderius had told Jorian that Abacarus had children of his own.

Sitting at a desk in the Academy, the philosopher made a steeple of his fingers, saying: "You wish me to evoke a demon and compel it to bring your wife forth from an underground cell in Xylar?"

"Aye, sir. Canst do it?"

"I believe so."

"What would that cost?"

Abacarus made notes on a waxed tablet with a stylus. After calculating, he said: "I'll undertake the task for fifteen hundred Othomaean nobles. I cannot guarantee success; I can only promise to do my best."

Jorian suppressed a temptation to whistle. "Let me borrow your tablet, Doctor. Let's see; in Penembian royals that would be...." He calculated and looked glumly at Karadur. "Had I but known, I'd have fetched a whole tubful of gold from Iraz."

"Gorax could not have borne the weight," Karadur protested.

"Can you pay?" asked Abacarus.

"Aye, though 'twill leave me nigh penniless. Why so much?"

"The spell requires rare ingredients, which will take at least a month to collect. Moreover, it is fraught with no small risk. Fifth Plane demons are formidable bondservants."

Jorian made a half-hearted effort to bargain Abacarus down, but the philosopher-sorcerer was adamant. At last Jorian said: "Shall we agree, half now and half when my wife is delivered to me unharmed?"

"That seems fair," said Gwiderius.

Abacarus cast a sour look at his colleague but grunted assent. Jorian counted out the money. Back at the Silver Dragon, he told Karadur:

"We'd better find ourselves livelihoods whilst waiting for Abacarus. Else we shall run out and be cast into the street. You can read palms or the like, whilst I seek work I can do."

Three days later, Jorian, having canvassed the city in vain for jobs in clock making and surveying, reported to Karadur that he had obtained a job in a windmill. Karadur had a new tale of woe.

"I found a booth for rent and made ready to hang out my sign," he said, "when a man of the local seers' guild appeared, with three bully boys. He told me, politely, that

48

I needs must join the guild, at twice the regular rate because of being a foreigner. Since his escort looked eager for a pretext to set upon me with fists and feet, I forwent argument, promising to pay ere I began practice."

"How much did they want?"

"Fifty nobles for the initiation fee, plus dues of one noble a quarter."

"At that rate, we shan't be able to pay Abacarus his second installment, unless the goddess Elidora suddenly smile upon us."

"You could sell your sword. Whilst I know little of weaponry, meseems it would fetch a substantial price."

"And then what should I do the next time a dragon or a band of rogues assail me? I have a better thought. Let's appeal to Goania. Surely she has influence with this seers' guild."

The next day, while Karadur went to see Goania, Jorian departed for his first day's work at the mill. The miller, an elderly Othomaean named Lodegar, explained that he was taking on Jorian because hitherto he and his wife had run the mill together. He trimmed the sails while the wife sat at the spout from the millstones and caught the flour in bags as it poured out. Now he was getting old for such gymnastics. His son, a soldier, could not help; so he would collect the flour while Jorian manned the sails.

Jorian had a vague idea that running a windmill was easy. One dumped the grain into the hopper, made a few adjustments for wind speed and direction, and waited for the flour to pour out.

The reality proved different. The wind was ever veering and backing, so that the turret bearing the sails had to be turned to face it. A circle of thick wooden pegs arose around the circular top of the tower, and the circumference of the turret bore a series of equally spaced holes on its inner surface. By thrusting a crowbar between the pegs and into one of the holes and heaving, one turned the turret a few degrees.

Outside, the main shaft of the turret bore four booms, crossing at the axis of the main shaft and thus providing spars to bear eight triangular sails, like a ship's jib. The clew of each sail was tied by a rope to the end of the adjacent boom. To shorten sail, one stopped the rotation of the booms by snubbing with a rope, unhitched the sail, wound it several times around its boom to lessen the area exposed to the wind, and tied the clew again to the end of the next boom in the circle. To spread sail, one reversed the operation.

Jorian was kept on the run all day. When the wind shifted direction, he had to man the crowbar to turn the turret. When it freshened, he scrambled down the ladder to stop the booms' rotation and shorten several of the jibs, lest the millstones, by spinning too fast, scorch the grain. When the wind died, he had to go down again to fly more sail, lest the machine grind to a halt. Between times, the miller directed him to lubricate the wooden shafting and gears with liquid soap, kept in a bucket and applied with a large paint brush.

During the morning, Jorian, bustling about in response to Lodegar's commands, tripped on the bucket and knocked it over. Liquid soap ran out over the floor and trickled between the boards into the base of the mill. Lodegar exploded:

"Vaisus smite you with emerods, ye clumsy oaf! Therius stiffen your joints and soften your prick! Go now to my house, get a bucket of water and some rags from my wife, and clean up this mess, or 'twill be too slippery to walk upon!"

The cleanup took hours, because Jorian had to leave it every few minutes to shift the bearing of the turret, or to descend the ladder to spread or shorten sail.

As night fell, Jorian returned to the Silver Dragon, barely able to put one foot before the other. He slumped down on a bench in the common room, too tired to climb the stair to his and Karadur's room. "Beer, Master Rhuys!" he croaked.

Karadur appeared. "Why Jorian, you look fatigued! Was the work at the mill exacting?"

"Nay; 'twas as light as tossing a feather from hand to hand. How fared you?"

"Goania summoned Nennio, the chief of the seers' guild. She persuaded him to agree that I pay my initiation fee in installments over a year. Further he would not abate his demands. She told me privily that the fifty nobles are mainly a bribe to the officers of the guild. No more than a tenth of the sum reaches the guild's coffers, the rest disappearing into the purses of Master Nennio and his henchmen."

"Why does not some disgruntled guild member bring an action against these larceners?"

Karadur glanced about and lowered his voice. "Because, she whispered, they turn over a portion to the Grand Duke, who therefore protects them in their peculations. But say it not aloud in Lord Gwitlac's demesne, an you value your health."

Jorian sighed. "No wonder the romancers write tales of imaginary commonwealths, where all are honest, industrious, sober, and chaste, since such a thing seems not to exist in the real world. Is the afterworld any more virtuous?"

Karadur shrugged. "We shall doubtless ascertain soon enough; or sooner yet, if you permit that restless tongue to betray us."

"I guard my utterances. If such a land of universal virtue existed, I fear 'twere somewhat dull to dwell in."

"We need not fear, Jorian, that such a reign of tedium will ever afflict us. Betimes some simple dullness were welcome!"

✠✠✠✠✠✠✠✠✠✠✠✠✠✠✠✠✠✠✠

IV

THE DEMON RUAKH

JORIAN BECAME HARDENED TO MILL WORK, SINCE HE WAS A powerful man, albeit somewhat softened by his life in Iraz. To one who had repaired clocks for a living, the mechanism was simple. Whenever the machine stopped, Jorian located the trouble before Lodegar did. One of the wooden gear teeth on the main shaft had come loose and jammed the gear, and Jorian quickly repaired it.

The month of the Eagle was well along when Abacarus sent word that he was ready to call up a demon from the Fifth Plane. The next evening, trudging through a light dusting of snow, Jorian and Karadur gathered in Abacarus's oratory. This was a small, circular room in one of the ornamental towers of the Philosophy Building of the Academy. They found the sorcerer marking a pentacle with chalk on the center of the floor, all the furniture having been moved aside. Holding the other end of the measuring string was Abacarus's apprentice, a weasel-like young man named Octamon.

"Keep back!" said Abacarus. "If you step on a line, you

will break the pentacle and release the demon ere he have accepted my commands. That might be the end of all of us."

They crowded back against the wall while the diagram was completed. The sorcerers inscribed a pentagram, or five-pointed star in the pentacle, a small circle inside the pentagram, and many symbols in the angles of these figures.

Octamon lit five thick black candles and placed them at the points of the star, where they burned with a weird green flame. Then he extinguished the suspended lamp that had illuminated the chamber. He lit a thuribulum and stood against the wall, swinging the vessel on its chain. Pungent odors arose, which called to Jorian's mind, simultaneously, a flowery spring meadow, the fish market at Vindium, and the tannery at Xylar. Glancing furtively at his companions' faces, Jorian saw that all were tinged green from the candle flames.

Abacarus began moving his hands while intoning, in a deep voice unlike his normal high, thin tenor, words unknown to Jorian: "*Thomatos benesser flianter, litan izer osnas nanther, soutram i ubarsinens rabiam! Siras etar besanar, nades suradis a....*" He went on and on until Jorian uneasily shifted his weight.

The flames of the candles wavered, shrank to points, and changed to an angry red. "*...maniner o sader prostas....*" droned Abacarus.

In the near-darkness, Jorian felt movement of the air. Something was flickering into view in the center of the pentacle; something anthropomorphic but bulkier than a human being. A heavy, musky odor pervaded the room. Abacarus finished his conjuration: "*...mammes i enaim perantes ra sonastos!* What is your name?"

The answer came in a voice like bubbling swamp gas: "If it be any of your business, I am called Ruakh. What is this outrage—"

"Hold your tongue!" said Abacarus. "I have called you from the Fifth Plane to perform a service. Until you swear by the oath that binds you to perform this task featly, and to harm no inhabitant of this plane whilst sojourning

53

therein, and then to return forthwith to your own plane,
you shall remain prisoner in this pentacle."

The dim form moved as if it were trying to break through
an invisible barrier surrounding it. The barrier seemed to
be elastic, so that when the being threw itself against the
invisible wall, it rebounded. At last it ceased its struggles,
saying:

"This is most unjust of you! On my plane we have long
abolished slavery, yet you savages still keep up this barbarous custom. Some day we demons shall find a
way—"

"Never mind all that," growled Abacarus. "Will you do
as you are told, or must I leave you here to await the
coming of day?"

"You beast!" said the demon. "You know we Fifth Planers be allergic to the sun of your plane. If ever I get you
on my plane—"

"Vaisus damn it, will you stop arguing! I have never
faced so contentious a demon! It will avail you nought,
so you might as well get down to business."

"I have a right to remind you of what is right and wrong,
since you seem to have no conscience—"

"*Shut up!*" screamed Abacarus.

"—and no manners, either," continued Ruakh. "Ah,
well, as you Prime Planers would say, you have me by the
balls, or would, if I had those repulsive organs of repro-
duction you creatures hide beneath your clothing. What
is this service?"

"First you must swear the oath!"

"I will swear nought until I know what service you
have in mind, lest you send me to find frog feathers or dry
water."

Abacarus said: "The large young man with the black
beard has a wife imprisoned in the dungeon of the royal
palace of Xylar. He wishes you to fetch her out of her cell
and bring her here."

"How far is Xylar?"

"Eighty leagues, more or less, east of here."

"How shall I accomplish this task? I can materialize in

the lady's cell, but I cannot dematerialize her to carry her through stone walls or an iron-barred door."

"If the door be locked, you must get the key from the head jailer, or whoever has it. If you can find who has it, you can easily frighten him into giving it up. Then you can fly back hither with the lady. The time is not yet midnight, so you should arrive here well before dawn. You must not fly at such a height that lack of air will suffocate her; and you should wrap her warmly, for the winter air aloft will be far below the freezing point."

Ruakh grunted. "I like not the prospect; but as we say on the Fifth Plane, mendicants cannot be optants. Can the young man draw me a plan of the dungeon, lest I go astray in the bowels of this building?"

"Nay, oath first! You hope he will break the circle and loose you to wreak your vengeance upon us."

"I had no such thought in mind!" cried the demon in its bubbly, thickly accented voice. "You Prime Planers are the most suspicious lot in the multiple worlds. You assume all others to be as evil and treacherous as you."

"Forget the rhetoric, my good Ruakh, and let us get to the oath."

"Oh, very well," grumbled the demon.

There followed a long dialogue between the two, in a language unknown to Jorian. At last Abacarus said: "That is done, then. Octamon, you may light the lamp and break the circle. You realize, Ruakh, what will befall you if you violate the terms of our compact, do you not?"

"Aye, I realize; albeit it is a monstrous injustice. Forcing me to do risky, unpaid labor, forsooth! When I get home, I shall have somewhat to say to my fellow demons."

As the lamp flared up, Jorian had his first clear view of Ruakh. The demon was a being of human size and shape, but from its back grew a huge pair of batlike wings, now folded. Its clawed feet resembled those of a huge bird of prey. The whole creature was covered with what at first Jorian took to be a skintight suit of scarlet silk. As the demon moved, he saw that this was Ruakh's own skin. As the being had said, it was innocent of visible sexual organs; the skin of its crotch was smooth.

"Pardon me, Master Ruakh," said Jorian, "but how *do* your kind reproduce themselves?"

"It is a long story," began the demon. "At the proper season, we grow—"

Abacarus interrupted. "Do not take time for such discussion, Master Jorian. Ruakh must get to Xylar and back ere dawn. So here is a piece of chalk; pray indicate where he shall find your lady."

Jorian squatted and drew a diagram of the dungeon of Xylar. He was a little startled when Ruakh, leaning over his shoulder to look at the drawing, placed a clawed hand on Jorian's back to steady itself. Jorian pointed to the largest rectangle in the diagram.

"I think she's in there," he said. "They seem to have fixed the place up for her comfort, not like an ordinary prison cell. She is small and light-haired."

The demon, peering, said: "Methinks I grasp the nub. Stand back, all, so that I can dematerialize."

When the men had crowded back to the wall, the demon began to spin round and round. Faster and faster it went, until it became a blur. The blur became translucent, then transparent, and then vanished with a *whoosh* of air.

"Open the doors, Octamon," said Abacarus, "to rid us of this stench."

Cold winter air spilled into the oratory. "Now what?" asked Jorian.

"It will be hours ere Ruakh can return," said Abacarus. "It can hie to Xylar in its immaterial form in the blink of an eye; it should arrive there any minute. But to return, it must remain material. So its flight will consume hours, swift of wing though it be. If you people wish to await its return here, there are couches below."

Jorian and Karadur remained in the Philosophy Building. As Abacarus was showing them to the lounge where they would pass the rest of the night, Jorian asked:

"Pray tell me something, Doctor Abacarus. In Iraz, a savant of the House of Learning explained that a flying being the size of a man were impossible. Something about the relation of is weight to the area of its wings and the power of its thews. How, then, can Ruakh fly in his material form on this plane?"

Abacarus shrugged. "It has compensating advantages. Its muscles are not made of the same stuff as ours. They are stronger in proportion to their bulk."

"What's this," said Jorian, "about the demons complaining of being enslaved by us Prime Planers? I thought the Novarian nations had agreed to end slavery."

Abacarus chuckled. "The Treaty of Metouro, which will not become effective until all twelve governments sign it, refers only to the enslavement of human beings. Demons, from whatever other plane, are not human and hence do not qualify, any more than would your horse."

"How about the ape-men of Komilakh? Will they count as human beings?"

"That depends on which of the twelve nations you are in. The courts of some have held them human; of others, not. The Novarian nations should establish a supreme court over all twelve systems to reconcile these discrepancies. I belong to a society devoted to this ideal; I must give you one of our broadsheets. But to return to the Treaty of Metouro, only five of the nations have signed it, and do not try to hold your breath whilst awaiting the signatures of the rest."

"What about the demons' threat to organize against exploitation by Prime Planers?"

"Never fear. They will make a start and then fall into internal bickering as they always have. Now I am going home. I shall return an hour before dawn. By then, if all go well, our demon should be well on its way hither. Good night!"

It seemed to Jorian that he had barely fallen asleep on his couch, when he felt his shoulder shaken. "It is time," said Abacarus.

Jorian stood yawning in the oratory for half an hour. Then, just as the east began to lighten, something moved against the star-strewn western sky. Abacarus threw open the doors that unfolded on the small balcony encircling the tower, letting in a wave of frigid air. The flying object took shape, growing from the likeness of a bat to the demon Ruakh with a bulky burden in its arms.

With a muffled thunder of wings, the demon settled upon the railing of the balcony, grasping it with clawed feet as a bird does a branch. Then, wings folded, it hopped down to the balcony and walked into the oratory, bearing a blanket-wrapped body. Octamon shut the door.

"Here you are!" growled the demon. The musky smell returned.

"Had you trouble getting in?" asked Jorian.

"Nay. I materialized outside the dungeon, thinking to get the keys. But I found the barred door at the head of the stair open, and a guard sitting beside it. I frightened him away, descended the stair, and found the cell whereof you told me, also unlocked. So I discovered this woman therein. When I approached her to explain my mission, she fainted. I wrapped her as you see and bore her out. The palace folk scattered shrieking before me, so I had no difficulty in leaving the building and taking to the air."

"Well done!" said Abacarus. "You are dismissed, Master Ruakh."

Ruakh gave a bubbling growl. "Ere I return to my own plane, let me tell you Prime Planers, we demons will not forever submit to being kidnapped and forced to run your errands for you! We shall unite to end this injustice! We shall overcome!"

"For now, be satisfied with your dismissal," said Abacarus. "Begone; we do not find your odor pleasing."

Standing in the center of the floor, Ruakh went into its spin. The towering scarlet form whirled, blurred, and vanished with a rush of displaced air.

Jorian drew a long breath. "I confess that Ruakh's proximity gave me some uneasy moments."

"It is all in knowing how to handle them," said Abacarus. "My last apprentice got himself slain by a demon whom he improperly evoked."

"Jorian is forever deprecating himself," said Karadur. "I have sought to break him of the habit, since modesty is a poor weapon for making one's way in this sinful world; but I fear I have not utterly succeeded."

Jorian was kneeling by the blanket-wrapped form on the floor. As he began unwrapping it, he was struck by the horrible thought that his Estrildis might have perished from mountain sickness at the altitude to which Ruakh had borne her.

Then the form began to wriggle, and it threw off the blanket and sat up.

"By Imbal's brazen balls!" cried Jorian. "You're not Estrildis!"

"Whoever said I was?" said the woman, rising. "I am Queen Estrildis's lady-in-waiting, Lady Margalit of Totens. And you, an I mistake not, are the fugitive King Jorian. Where am I, and why have I been brought on this horrible journey?"

The woman was of about the same age as Estrildis; but there the resemblance ended. Where Estrildis was short and blond, Margalit of Totens was almost as tall as Jorian and dark, with a mop of curly hair tumbling over her forehead. Jorian would not quite have called her beautiful, as he would have said of some of the five wives he had enjoyed as king. But she was handsome in a bold, sharp-featured way, and strongly built. She was fast recovering from the shock of her experience.

Jorian bowed. "I am honored, Lady Margalit. You are in Othomae City, and it was not intended that you be brought hither. I sent Ruakh—that's the demon—to fetch my wife, but he seems to have caught you by mistake. How did it happen?"

"My Queen had gone up to the battlements to walk and look at the heavens, leaving me in our dungeon apartment."

"They don't keep her locked in that cell, then?"

"Nay, though they make sure she leaves not the palace. She may issue from the cell when she pleases, but they send an armed escort with her, lest you have another try at abducting her."

"Was it you who gave the alarm, when I fell over that chair and roused the watchdog?"

"Aye. How was I to know it was you?"

"Why told you not the demon who you were?"

59

"How could I? I was tidying up the apartment in Estrildis's absence—as you doubtless know, neatness was never her strong point—and the first thing I knew, there was the demon in the doorway, crouching to get his wings through, and mumbling something in that gargly voice with its unintelligible accent. 'Twas then that I fainted for the only time in my life. The next I knew, I was borne aloft, wrapped in this blanket, notwithstanding which I well-nigh froze to death. When I struggled, the demon warned me to lie still, lest he drop me from a height. What an experience!"

Jorian turned to Abacarus. "How could Ruakh have made such a stupid mistake? I told him to look for a small, blond woman."

The sorcerer spread his hands. "By and large, demons are not very intelligent. Belike it forgot your instructions, or got them confused, and when it saw one woman alone in the chamber reasoned that this must be she whom it sought."

"Can you call Ruakh back to rectify his error?" asked Jorian.

"Nay. A demon once dismissed is exempt for years thereafter."

"Why did you dismiss him so hastily?"

"Because it stank, and you did not object."

"I had no time to object; but let's not start apportioning blame. Could you invoke another demon in Ruakh's place?"

Abacarus frowled. "Not for months. Imprimus, these evocations are exhausting, and I must be able to meet my classes. I also find the odor of Fifth Plane demons unbearable. Secundus, it would cost you an additional fifteen hundred nobles. And tertius, you have not yet paid all you owe me for evoking Ruakh."

"What!" cried Jorian. "I owe you not a copper penny! We agreed that your demon should fetch my wife, Estrildis the Kortolian; and that he has not done."

"Young man, you had better watch your tongue. I say you owe me seven hundred and fifty. My expenses have been just as heavy as if the demon had succeeded, and I warned you that I did not guarantee success."

"But you did agree to my paying the rest when and only when you succeeded. I'll not pay for a bungled job!"

"You were as responsible for the bungle as anyone, and you had better pay. I can take you to law; and I also have other means of causing you trouble."

"Try it!" said Jorian. "Come on, Karadur. An I ever resort to sorcery again, I'll try to find a sorcerer who is at least both competent and honest."

"What of me?" cried Margalit. "Am I expected to walk back to Xylar? By Zevatas's whiskers, my Lord Jorian, were we both in Xylar, I'd sue you within a digit of your life."

"I beg your pardon, my lady. Come to our hostelry, and we'll discuss your future."

Back at the Silver Dragon, Jorian engaged a private room for Margalit, whose initial anger had cooled. He told her:

"Certes, I am obligated to get you back to Xylar. But you cannot travel thither alone, especially at this time of year, when packs of wolves and bands of robbers are desperate for food. I cannot afford to hire a proper escort and procure animals to carry you. And I cannot accompany you into Xylar myself if I wish to keep my head attached to the rest of me."

"I cannot blame you for that," she said. "Like my Queen, I have turned against this custom, venerable though it be."

Jorian continued: "So I will pay your keep here as long as my money holds out. When spring comes, some means of conveying you, such as a diligencia or a merchants' caravan, will surely turn up. Now you'd better get some sleep."

"What next, Your Majesty?" said Margalit.

"I pray, do *not* call me that, even in sarcasm! I never wanted to be king of your preposterous country, and ever since my escape I've been trying to divest myself of the honor. But to answer your question: I must away to my job at the mill. Tonight at dinner, we'll consider what to do. I'll summon the wizardess Goania, who has more sense than most."

Margalit looked down at her gown. "I am no glass of

fashion, but I shall really need at least one change of clothing. Without washing, this garment will become as odorous as your demon, and I cannot run about naked whilst it is being cleansed."

"In winter, anyway," said Jorian. "I suppose your abductor gave you no time to snatch up a purse?"

"You suppose rightly, Your M— Master Jorian."

Jorian sighed and took two pieces of gold from his purse. "I know nought of the cost of ladies' garments, but see what you can do with this. Get Karadur to go with you."

That evening, as they sat at table waiting for Goania, Margalit said: "You certainly seem determined, Master Jorian. You've vainly tried a direct attack, and then sorcery, in your efforts to obtain my Queen; but you still have not given up."

"That's true love," said Jorian. "I'm not ashamed of it. She's the one I chose for myself, not picked for me by the Council to give the leading magnates a stake in my rule. And she's the one I want."

"When and if you recover her, what then?"

"Why, we'll find some safe place, whence the Xylarians cannot snatch me, and settle down as a proper tradesman and wife to earn a living."

"You may find her changed."

Jorian dismissed the idea with a wave. "Were she old, wrinkled, and gray, she would still be my true love."

Karadur chuckled. "My boy is a sentimental romanticist," he said, wagging his vast, white beard. "Do not try to change him, Lady Margalit; for it is one of his attractive qualities. Ah, here comes my eminent colleague!"

The wizardess Goania, followed by her bodyguard Boso, entered. Jorian, relieved to see that Vanora was not with them, made introductions. Goania said:

"Welcome, Lady Margalit. When I saw you, I wondered what magic could have changed you from a short blonde, as Jorian has described his Estrildis, into a tall brunette. What befell?"

When Jorian and Margalit had told their stories, Goania said: "Never underestimate the stupidity of demons. Those from most of the other planes have powers that on this plane appear preternatural. Are you familiar with the theory that every life form is descended from others, all going back to some little blob of primordial slime?"

"Aye," said Jorian. "When I studied here under Gwiderius, a professor was dismissed from the Academy for such ungodly speculations."

"Well, this theory explains the stupidity of most demons. Having these powers, the stress of competition on their own respective planes has not forced them to develop their mental powers to the degree that we, who can neither fly, nor make ourselves invisible, nor dematerialize, have been forced to do.

"I can give an example from my own experience. When I was a mere girl—stare not, Master Jorian; I was once young and quite as pretty as your Estrildis."

"Very well, Aunt Goania. I believe you."

"When I was, as I say, a maiden, I had a suitor named Uriano, who dabbled, unbeknownst to me, in sorcery. This was ere I myself decided to make occult pursuits my life's work. I expected to wed, keep house, and bear brats like most women; and I was sore assotted with Uriano, for he was a handsome devil.

"My father, a building contractor, had no use for Uriano, terming him a lecher, a wastrel, a dabbler, and generally worthless. Anon I learned that Uriano was all those things; but then my eyes, blinded by love, were closed to them. My sire barred my sweet swain from the house and forbade me to have aught to do with him.

"I wept, carried on, and made a great to-do; for I deemed myself the victim of a monstrous injustice, inflicted by one grown so old as to have forgotten the joys of youthful love and filled with blind prejudice against the newer and more enlightened views of the younger generation. But relent my father would not.

"Uriano, howsomever, discovered that, by skulking through some shrubbery that grew nigh our house, he could approach within twenty paces of the edifice unseen, on the side of my bedchamber. So we presently began communicating by his shooting headless arrows from a child's toy bow, with messages wrapped around them, through my open window. I wrote replies, tied them to the arrows, and threw them back.

"Then Uriano proposed that we elope. I, foolish girl, assumed he meant to hale me to the Temple of Therius and make me his lawful wife. From what I heard later, I'm sure he meant only to enjoy my body until he tired of me and cast me adrift.

"On a certain night, he said, he would appear with a ladder, down which I should descend into his arms, and away we should fly. What he did not tell me was that, in his sorcerous experiments, he had evoked a demon from the Seventh Plane to help him. Seventh Plane demons are fiery beings, particularly dangerous for a tyronic, unskilled sorcerer to handle.

"On the appointed night, Uriano came with his ladder, accompanied by his demon. He placed the ladder against the wall and charged the demon to cover our retreat when, as he thought, we should flee from the house together. He posted the demon at the back door, with orders to incinerate with his fiery breath anyone who came through that door ere we were out of sight of the house. Then the demon should rejoin his master.

"All might have gone as planned but for two things. Imprimus, so crazed with lust was Uriano from thinking of his future leman that he could not wait until we left the house to slake it. Instead of signaling and waiting for me to descend the ladder, which I could easily have done, he climbed the ladder himself to enter my bedchamber through the window, hoping to take me featly then and there before departure.

"Secundus, in emplacing the ladder, he did not set the base far enough from the wall. So as he climbed from the topmost rung through the window, he unwittingly kicked the ladder over.

"When he heard the ladder strike the ground, all thought of carnal congress fled his mind, unhoused by fears for his own safety. He whispered: 'Be quiet, dear one, and I'll soon set this picklement to rights.' Then he leaned out the window and softly called: 'Vrix! O Vrix!'

"'Aye, Master?' said the demon from below.

"'Pick up that ladder and set it against the house, as it was.'

"'Eh?' said the demon. 'What sayst?'

"Uriano repeated his command, but the demon could not seem to understand this simple act. First it set the ladder on edge along the ground. Then it raised the ladder and set it on end, away from the house and unsupported. When it released its hold, the ladder naturally fell over.

"After more blunders, Vrix finally seemed to understand. But as I said, these demons are fiery beings. As it came anigh the house with the ladder, the ladder caught fire from the heat of the demon's grasp. As the demon set it in place, it blazed up merrily, and Uriano had to push it over again to keep it from firing the house.

"'Gods!' quotha. 'That stupid oaf—but now we must needs go out through the house. Does your sire sleep?'

"'I think so,' I said. I opened my bedroom door and looked down the hall, hearing nought. I beckoned Uriano, and together we tiptoed to the head of the stair.

"Just then the door of my parents' room opened, and there stood my father in his nightshirt, blinking, with a candle in one hand and a sword in the other. 'What's all this infernal noise—' he began. Then, recognizing Uriano, he rushed roaring at him.

"Uriano let go my hand and bounded down the stairs two at a time, with my sire after him. The speed of my father's motion extinguished the candle, but there was still enough moonlight to see one's way.

"Uriano dashed through the dining room into the kitchen and out the back door. Vrix stood there, waiting for someone to come out that door. When Uriano appeared, Vrix gave him a blast of fiery breath that washed over him like a jet of water from a fountain in the Grand Duke's gardens, for it had been straitly commanded to burn the first person coming out. Uriano gave one shriek as his hair and clothing blazed up, and then there was nought left of him but a black, cindery mass on the garden path. Uriano's death released Vrix from servitude on this plane, and it vanished. So now I hope you appreciate the limitations of employing demons to do your work for you."

"I realize the difficulty," said Jorian. "But what interests me most is the question of what would have happened, had your lover not knocked over the ladder?"

"Oft have I asked myself that question," said Goania. "Things would in time have gone ill, I am certain." She sighed, with a faraway look. "But I should have had one interesting night to remember."

Jorian said: "But still, can you think of a better way to get my darling out of her luxurious lockup?"

"Not at the moment."

"Could you send your second sight to Xylar, to see what they are doing there?"

"I could, if someone will clean this table and fetch me a clean glass."

Goania repeated her previous trance, the one she had employed after Jorian and Karadur had just emerged from jail. When she spoke, she muttered:

"I cannot see inside the palace...there seems to be a barrier....It is like a wall of glass, shutting me out....I see the palace dimly and wavering, as things appear to ripple when seen above a paved road on a hot day....Nay, I cannot get in."

After a while she opened her eyes and said: "The Xylarians have thrown a magical barrier around their palace, like a dome, which keeps out my occult vision. From what I know of such things, I am sure it would also keep out any demon who tried to enter in dematerialized form."

"I suppose," said Jorian, "that after Ruakh's visit they hired a spooker to set up this barrier against further intrusions. What shall I do now?"

"I would start looking for another wife, if you must have one," said Goania.

"Aye," Karadur chimed in. "Relinquish this hopeless quest, my son, ere you bring destruction not only on yourself but also on others, like me."

"You may go your way any time," snapped Jorian. "You are not my bondservant."

"Oh, my dear Jorian! I have become dependent upon you. I am too old and creaky to get about much by myself. Cast me not off like an old shoe! You take the place of the son I never had."

"Very well then, you must needs put up with my vagaries. The single life may suit you and Goania, but it pleases me not."

"If you must have a wife, then, follow Goania's rede. Wed—let me see—why not take Lady Margalit here?"

"Come!" said Margalit sharply. "I am not a prize to be raffled off. Master Jorian may be a fine fellow in his way—"

"But obstinate as a mule when he gets an idea in his mazard," Karadur put in.

"—but there is nought like that betwixt us."

"Do you expect to wed someday?" Goania asked.

"Certes. That's why I took the post of lady-in-waiting. My family, though of good lineage, is poor; so by saving up the allowance the Regency pays me, I hoped to gather enough dowry to lure some reasonably whole, sane, and solvent husband. But my peculum lies still in Estrildis's dungeon apartment."

"Well, then—" said Karadur.

"I must know and like the fellow far better than I do Jorian ere I'd consider such a thing. Besides, he is already bespoken."

"Good for you!" said Jorian. "But as the doctor says, I can be very stubborn. You two spookers are ever talking of the wisdom your years have brought you. So let's have evidence, in the form of a plausible scheme for recovering my wife!"

All four sat in silence. Rhuys brought their dinners. As they were digging in, Karadur said:

"I once told you of a Mulvanian colleague, called Greatsoul Shenderu or Shenderu the Wise. He dwells on Mount Aravia in the Lograms, and such is his name for wisdom that folk come hundreds of leagues to consult him on their affairs. Belike you could seek him out, come spring."

"A splendid suggestion!" cried Jorian, his normal enthusiasm returning. "Why thought you not of that sooner? I'll set out forthwith!"

"Oh, Jorian!" said Goania. "Rush not into needless peril, or your Estrildis may have no husband to rejoin. It's still the month of the Eagle, and the snows lie heavy on the mountains."

"Methinks we've seen the last of the snow down here," said Jorian.

"Down here is not up there. There you'll find drifts as deep as you are tall, with crevasses and precipices."

"I know; we flew over the Lograms coming from Iraz. But I'll chance that. Doctor Karadur, how does this Shenderu live?"

"People who come with questions are expected to recompense him with the things he requires: food, firewood, and betimes a garment or some knicknack such as a cooking pot. Since he is a vegetarian, his alimentary requirements are bulky."

"I'll buy a mule and load it with firewood, bread, and turnips," said Jorian. "I'll persuade Gwiderius to gain me access to the Grand Ducal library, where they'll have maps of the region. I shall be off ere the month be out!"

As often happens, it took Jorian much longer to get his expedition ready to go than he had thought. He had to buy a horse and a pack mule with the remains of King Ishbahar's privy purse. He needed a load of grain for the animals, since there would be little natural forage for them at that season.

Then a minor epidemic swept Othomae City with coughs, sneezes, and fevers. All the people in the Silver Dragon, including Jorian, were out of effective action for a sennight.

As the month of the Boar wore on, Lady Margalit became impatient with idleness. One night over dinner, Jorian was counting out his remaining coin.

"At this rate," he said, "I shall be a pauper by summer. It's only right that I should pay Margalit's room and board, since I brought her hither. But with the pittance Lodegar pays me, I cannot save, scrimp though I try."

Margalit said: "Jorian, it is good of you to pay my board; but I should earn something on my own. Could I not find a paying place in Othomae until arrangements are made for my return?"

Jorian raised his eyebrows. "Lady Margalit! One of your kind could hardly be a housemaid or a washerwoman."

"What mean you, my kind? I've known poverty, and I'm not too proud to do what must be done. Besides, much of what I did for Estrildis would elsewhere be housemaid's work."

"I'll ask Goania," said Jorian.

When Lodegar fell sick of the same phthisic, Jorian persuaded him to hire Margalit to take his place in the mill, bagging the flour as it came from the millstones. A few days later, as they returned to the Silver Dragon after work, still patting flour from each other's garments, Goania greeted them.

"I have a post for you, Lady Margalit," she said. "My friend Aeda, wife of Councilor Arvirag, needs a maid-of-all-work, hers having left. What say you?"

"I will certainly try it," said Margalit.

"Good girl!" said Jorian. "I admire anyone willing to turn his hand to what needs doing. I hope we can find you a position which shall make better use of that excellent brain of yours. Meanwhile, let's celebrate with a bottle of Rhuys's best!"

They were halfway through the bottle, and Rhuys had served their dinners, when a man entered the common room and strode up to Jorian. The man, wearing a uniform without a sword, said: "You are Jorian of Ardamai, alias Nikko of Kortoli?"

"Aye," said Jorian. "What about it?"

"Here is a summons to appear before the examining magistrate one hour after sunrise on the morrow."

"Eh? What?" said Jorian. "What have I done?"

"You are the defendant in an action brought by Doctor Abacarus of the Academy, for recovery of a debt."

69

"That bastard!" muttered Jorian.

"Since you are a foreigner, you must either get a local citizen and property owner to vouch for you, or you must come with me to the jail, to assure your appearance tomorrow."

"I will vouch for him," said Goania.

"So? Then kindly sign here, Mistress Goania."

The process server departed, leaving the summons on the table before Jorian. Goania said: "I trust you know, Jorian, that if you lose your case, it's debtor's prison."

"Do they still have that here? When I was King of Xylar, I got them to abolish it, on the ground that a man in jail cannot earn the wherewithal to satisfy his debt."

"It is a pity that you are not the Grand Duke here. But you are not, so govern your acts accordingly."

The examining magistrate was the same Judge Flollo who had incarcerated Jorian and Karadur. He said: "Master Jorian, methinks that, having gotten out of trouble once, you would have sense enough to stay out. But let me hear your stories. You first, Doctor Abacarus."

Abacarus gave a long, voluble speech affirming his claim that Jorian still owed him 750 nobles. Jorian explained why he did not consider himself so obligated.

"Therefore," he said, "I ask that this suit be dismissed with prejudice. In fact, I ought to sue the learned doctor for my first seven hundred and fifty, since his effort was a complete failure."

"Nonsense!" said Abacarus. "I did not guarantee success, and I warned this upstart...."

Both the doctor and Jorian began shouting, until the magistrate banged his gavel and yelled: "Silence, you two, on pain of imprisonment! This is a hard case, the more so since neither of you has a written contract. One would think that men of your age would have sense enough to put such things in writing, with competent legal advice.

"Now, our calendar is crowded. The earliest trial date I can set is—let me see...." He ruffled through documents. " 'Twill be the fourteenth of the Dragon."

"By Heryx's brazen balls, that's half a year away!" exclaimed Jorian.

Judge Flollo shrugged. "It is the best we can do. Time, as the philosophers at the Academy are wont to say, is incompressible. Of course, if you two should settle out of court, no trial would be needed. Master Jorian, Mistress Goania's avouchment will suffice to leave you at liberty pending the trial. But you must understand that, if you fail to appear and we cannot catch you, the penalty will fall upon her."

Jorian and Abacarus exchanged glares. The sorcerer said: "My resources are not yet exhausted, Master Jorian."

"Nor mine," said Jorian.

Two nights later, Jorian had snuffed the candle in the room he shared with Karadur and stretched himself out beneath the blankets, when he became aware of something else in the room. Out of the darkness a luminous form was taking shape. At first it was so faint that he thought it a mere photism—one of the lights one sees with one's eyes closed. It wavered and shimmered with a faint bluish radiance, resembling a cowled figure. Nothing but blackness could be seen beneath the cowl where its face should be. Then came a moaning voice: "Pay your debts! Pay your debts!"

"Karadur!" said Jorian. "Wake up! Do you see what I see?"

"Unh?" The aged Mulvanian sat up and yawned. "Oh, ah, aye, I see it. This is termed a dunning specter, sent by Abacarus to plague us. 'Tis patent that he is not fain to wait till the month of the Dragon for the decision on his case."

"Pay your debts! Pay your debts!" wailed the figure.

"What should I do about it?" asked Jorian.

"There is naught much that you can do, short of paying Abacarus his claim."

"That I will not do. Even if I wished, I do not have seven hundred and fifty nobles left. What about these specters? What can they do?"

"These entities inhabit the Second Plane. They are easy to invoke and harmless, since they do not achieve substantial materialization on this plane. Whilst not intelligent, they are obedient to the sorcerer's commands, like a well-trained dog. The thing is immaterial, so your sword would pass through it without resistance. A project at the House of Learning in Iraz was to ascertain how, without forming solid vocal organs, these specters could natheless agitate the air of this plane to form articulate sounds—"

"Pay your debts! Pay your debts!"

"Well," said Jorian, "'tis damned inconvenient. The thing I most look forward to in the world is my first night after Estrildis and I are again united. But imagine how it would be if, just as she and I prepared to enjoy our mutual passion, this thing appeared with its croak!"

"At least," said Karadur, "this entity will assist you to adhere to the continence on which you have virtuously resolved."

"Oh, bugger my continence! Will it go on like this all night?"

"Pay your debts! Pay your debts!" groaned the specter.

"Nay," said Karadur. "After a few hours it will become fatigued and fade away—until the next night."

"Pay your debts! Pay your debts!"

"You are a great bore, spook!" growled Jorian. "Now shut your gob and go away!"

He pulled the covers over his head; but for the next hour or two, moans and wails of "pay your debts!" kept him awake.

The next day, since Lodegar's mill was idle for want of grain, Jorian went to Goania. He said: "I am no light-hearted manslayer, but I have punctured a few knaves in my time. If I could get within a sword's length of Abacarus—" He gripped his hilt, secured to the scabbard by peace wires.

"Do not even think of it, boy!" snapped Goania.

Jorian smiled. "I like to think of you as my favorite

aunt. And why should I not let some of the stuffing out of this great child's doll?"

"Because the Grand Duke's police keep a sharp eye on you, even if you are not aware thereof. You would only end up on the headsman's block, not to mention the trouble you would cause your friends."

"Well then, have you any sort of counter-sorcery against him?"

She pondered. "Aye, I can call up a similar specter from the Second Plane to harass Abacarus. But think twice! First, 'twill cost you money, albeit I am willing to let that debt ride until you can afford to pay. Secondly, Abacarus is an able wizard. He can throw a protective shield about his abode, like that which the Xylarians put up against my second sight."

"Does it bother Abacarus to erect and maintain these shields?"

"To some degree. They consume psychic energy."

"Then by all means send a dunning specter against him. Tell it to say: 'Cease your extortions!'"

Goania promised. Next day she told Jorian: "As I said, my specter had barely begun to harass Abacarus when he threw a shield about his chambers in the Academy. When he went home in the even, it followed him, intoning its message; but when he reached his house, he soon erected another shield against it."

"Can he make a private shield around himself, that shall move with him?"

"Nay. These shields must needs be anchored in soil or in a fixed abode."

"Well then, keep it after him when he goes betwixt his home and his oratory."

The next evening, Jorian idled in the cold, crisp air, along the path outside the Philosophy Building of the Academy. Weird blue lights flickered in the windows of Doctor Abacarus's tower, so Jorian knew the sorcerer was still at work. At length the lights went out, and soon Abacarus issued from the building.

Behind a tree, Jorian watched as the wizard strode along

the campus path, his vast belly bobbing. Presently a dunning specter like that which harassed Jorian appeared close behind Abacarus and began to howl: "Cease your extortions! Cease your extortions!"

Abacarus turned. Jorian could not see his expression, since the near-darkness was relieved only by starlight and the feeble glow of an oil lamp on a bracket beside the main door of the building. But the sorcerer made gestures, and Jorian's own dunning specter appeared, wailing: "Pay your debts!"

A clutch of undergraduates came along the path. They halted, and Jorian heard one say: "Great Zevatas, here's a duel of wizards! This should be fun to watch!"

"If they do not blow up the whole Academy in their strife," said another.

"I fear no spooks!" said still another. "I'll show you!" The youth picked up a stone and hurled it at Jorian's phantom. The stone passed through the specter without resistance and struck Jorian in the chest.

"Ho!" roared Jorian, grabbing his unusable sword. He started toward the group, who scampered away and disappeared. When Jorian turned back, Abacarus had also vanished. Jorian set out for the Silver Dragon, with the specter hovering over his shoulder and moaning: "Pay your debts!"

During the next fortnight, Jorian continued to be haunted by Abacarus's sending, while Goania's dunning specter harassed Abacarus as opportunity offered. The sorcerer, Jorian learned, found it necessary to change his habits. A night worker, he took to keeping farmer's hours, up with the dawn and home ere sunset, so as not to be caught abroad at night away from the protection of his shields.

Jorian found other resources in the campaign of mutual harassment. He hired urchins to paint ABACARUS IS AN EXTORTIONIST on the walls of the Philosophy Building. He hired a beggar to stroll about the campus bearing a sign reading ABACARUS IS AN EXTORTIONIST. When the campus police tried to arrest the beggar, a gang of undergraduates took the oldster's side and started a small riot, under cover of which the beggar slipped away.

When Abacarus filed a suit for damages against Jorian for harassment, Jorian filed a countersuit alleging the same tort. Judge Flollo looked sourly at the two litigants, saying:

"We cannot schedule these trials until next year. Why do not you two go to some barbarous land where dueling is legal, or trial by combat, and have it out?"

As the month of the Bull came on, Doctor Gwiderius told Jorian: "My colleague Abacarus wishes me to tell you that he is willing to discuss a compromise."

So Jorian found himself again in Abacarus's office in the Academy, facing the stout sorcerer across a huge desk. Abacarus said:

"Come, my good Jorian, this is no way for mature men to behave. Let us find a *modus vivendi*, ere the lawyers suck us dry. Otherwise we shall spend more on legal and court fees than the sum at issue."

"Well, sir?" said Jorian.

"Would you consider settling for half?"

"Never. Methinks it's plain, by all Novarian laws—the which I have studied—that I owe you not a copper penny more than I've paid. In fact, a clever lawyer could make a good case for the return of the seven hundred fifty I paid you erstwhile."

"If that idea pleases you not, have you a proposal to offer?"

Jorian thought. "How about submitting our dispute to an impartial arbitrator? Loser to pay the arbitrator's fee."

Abacarus pursed his lips and twiddled his fat fingers. "Not bad. We have some retired judges in Othomae, who could be counted upon to render a just verdict."

"Oh, no!" said Jorian. "An Othomaean judge would be prejudiced in your favor, since I am a foreigner. I should prefer a Kortolian judge; I am sure—"

"Rubbish! With our Othomaean judges, at least I have some notion of their fairness. But I know nought of Kortolian justice. For aught I know, any of your people were willing and eager to take a bribe to find for you."

75

"Kortolian justice is every bit as just as yours!"

"Belike, but how shall you prove it? Must we fight it out, as Flollo suggested? If you challenge me, I will naturally choose magical spells as the weapons."

"How about this?" said Jorian. "If I can find a jurist of high repute from a third Novarian state, will you accept him?"

"I would consider it with a favoring mind. I should have to make inquiries ere deciding. And this time, let us put our undertaking in writing!"

Jorian rose. "I agree. Let's leave it at that. Meanwhile, if you will banish your dunning specter, I will call off mine, as well as my other partisans. Whilst I fear not your phantom, it does make a good night's sleep hard to come by!"

V

THE SNOWS OF ARAVIA

Nᴏᴛ ᴛɪʟʟ ᴛʜᴇ ꜱᴇᴄᴏɴᴅ ᴏꜰ ᴛʜᴇ ʙᴜʟʟ ᴡᴀꜱ ᴊᴏʀɪᴀɴ ʀᴇᴀᴅʏ ᴛᴏ go. In the evening, he was packing his gear when a knock announced Vanora.

"Jorian," she said, "you are a fool to undertake this journey alone. You need at least one extra pair of eyes to watch for dangers, and an extra pair of hands to pull you out of quicksands and other traps."

"You may be right," said Jorian. "But, alas, I know no one here suitable. Doctor Karadur is too old and feeble. Your friend Boso has barely brain enough to tie his own shoe laces, besides which he loves me not."

"I could go," she said. "I'm strong, and as you well know, I've roughed it ere this."

Jorian shook his head. "Nay, my dear; I've been all through that. Your body may be up to the task, but I fear that your temper be too stormy and uncertain for me. I thank you for the offer."

"Be not a fool, Jorian! You need someone, and I'm the only one to hand. Your tale of a curse on your prick was

77

but a farrago to frighten me; Goania says such a spell were impossible."

"I am trying to tell you, I don't wish a female companion save my wife!"

"Oh, that little farm bitch! Forget her. When you win to her, you'll find one of the local lads has been tupping your prize ewe. After all, you and she have been apart now for over two years—"

"You had better go back to Boso and let me get on with my packing," growled Jorian.

"Look, Jorian darling, you need not bed me along the way if you're not fain to do so—"

"Curse it, Vanora, get out! Will you go, or must I throw you out?"

"You mangy scrowle!" she yelled. Jorian ducked as a shoe came flying at his head. "I'll teach you to cast off an honest woman!" A second shoe followed.

The door opened, and Boso's broad face looked in. "What in the nine hells goes on here?"

"He tried to rape me!" screamed Vanora, looking about for something more to throw.

"What!" roared Boso. "You lure my woman up here, and when she won't go with you, you ravish her? I'll teach you to steal honest men's women!"

"She lies!" shouted Jorian. "It was not—" Then he had to defend himself against Boso's bull-like rush. In an instant, they were floundering about, punching and kicking. A chair went over with a crash.

Feet pounded on the stair, and Rhuys looked in. "Here, here!" he said. "Stop that! If you're fain to fight, take your quarrel outside!"

When they paid no heed, Rhuys vanished but soon reappeared, armed with a bung starter and followed by his two sons and the stable boy. Boso had Jorian's head in the crook of his arm and was striving to punch Jorian's face with his free fist, while Jorian tried to block Boso's blows and to kick his shins.

"Seize them!" cried Rhuys.

The four newcomers grabbed the combatants and tried to pull them apart. They failed, because Jorian and Boso were both large, strong men. Suddenly Boso released Jorian's head and turned to throw a wild swing at the stable boy. The blow hurled the youth back against the wall. Rhuys and his sons pounced upon Boso. While the sons clung to Boso's arms, Rhuys whacked him over the head with the bung starter. Boso subsided. Jorian stood back, breathing hard, with bruises on his face and blood running from a cut lip.

"What befell?" asked Rhuys.

Sitting on the floor, Boso wagged his head and mumbled. Jorian began: "Mistress Vanora came up to have words with me, and Boso thought—"

"He lies!" screeched Vanora. "Jorian tried to rape me, and Boso came to my aid!"

"It was just the opposite!" shouted Jorian. "She besought me—"

"Quiet, both of you!" said Rhuys. To one of the sons he said: "Baltho, run and fetch Mistress Goania. She'll soon find out by her arcane arts who's lying." To Vanora he added: "I shan't be stonished if Master Jorian has the right of it. We've had trouble with you two before."

"Come on, Boso," said Vanora, taking the stout man by the arm. "They're all against us. Everyone hates us." She hauled him to his feet, and the pair went unsteadily out. As she left, she spat at Jorian: "I hate you!"

"Come back, Baltho!" Rhuys called after his son. "The wizardess will not be needed."

"There's your answer," said Jorian to Rhuys. "Now may I get on with my packing? God den, Lady Margalit!"

The lady-in-waiting appeared in the doorway. "What's all this direful noise?"

"Master Rhuys will explain," said Jorian. "As for me, I must be off ere daylight; so pray excuse me." Rhuys and his young men filed out.

Margalit shrugged. "I merely wished to ask if you would mind my sending a letter to my Queen, telling her I am well and will return when I can? A courier departs on the morrow for Xylar, and I can send it by him."

"Hm," murmured Jorian. "I mind not your reassuring her; but I crave not to have my present roost revealed.

79

Else we shall have a squad of Shvenic lariat men come to drag me off for an over-close haircut."

"I could say I wrote from Vindium or Govannian."

"Ah, but if anyone question the courier, he'll tell whence he brought the letter." Jorian frowned. "I have it! Write your letter, without saying whence it comes. I'll inclose it in a letter to my mother in Kortoli, wherein I shall ask her to send the inclosed epistle to Xylar by the next courier."

Margalit sighed. "At that rate, with postal service in its present parlous plight, my letter will not be delivered until summer. By then my position may have gone to another. But I feel responsible to my Queen for you. She'd not thank me for getting her a headless husband."

"Neither should I," said Jorian. "Not that a head ever has much to say after it has been sundered from its body. The operation impairs clear thinking."

"If you are leaving early," said Margalit, "I must write my letter forthwith."

Three days after leaving Othomae, Jorian arrived at the inn recommended to him, the Golden Ibex. This inn stood on a secondary road in the foothills of the Lograms. Over the nearer hills could be seen the snowclad peak of Aravia.

Jorian rode the horse he had bought. This was a middle-aged gelding, useless for mounted combat or desperate chases; but Jorian hoped he would not need a mount for such purposes, and this animal had been for sale cheap. Jorian named the horse Fimbri, after a carpenter to whom he had once been apprenticed. He led the mule, which he called Filoman, after a notably foolish former King of Kortoli.

"The trail to Aravia leaves the road here," said the taverner, Turonus. "I would not try to ride a horse up to old Shenderu's cave, for the latter part of the journey is too steep and rocky, and the snow too deep. If ye walk leading your pack mule, ye should do all right, an ye fear not the ghost of Captain Oswic."

"What's that tale?"

"In my grandsire's time, they say, Oswic led a band of

brigands in these parts, terrorizing the land for leagues around. At last the Grand Bastard, that was then, sent a company of soldiery against Oswic. They trailed him and his band up the slopes of Mount Aravia, until they reached a level place overlooking a steep slope. Here Oswic and his men chose to make a stand; for they outnumbered the soldiers. Moreover, beyond that point the slope became too steep for riding, and they would have had to abandon their horses and struggle up the slope afoot, belike to be picked off by archers in the open.

"Oswic made a fiery speech, that 'twere better to die on their feet than to live on their knees; and that whereas death in battle was a possibility, it was a certainty if the soldiers laid hands upon them. Then he flourished his sword and led a charge down upon the soldiers.

"The banditti were well armed, and after the first shock the soldiers began to give way. But then Oswic raised his sword on high in an inspiriting gesture and began a shout of victory. So intent was he upon harkening on his men that he failed to guard himself. A soldier rode up behind him and smote off Captain Oswic's head, which went rolling down the slope, bumping the bases of trees and rolling on. Some of the soldiers swore that the severed head continued to shout exhortations to the robbers; but I misdoubt this. Without lungs to blow air through the vocal organs, how could a head cry out?

"So fell a fighter, howsomever, was Captain Oswic that the headless body continued to wave its sword to encourage the brigands and to strive to smite the troopers. But, lacking eyes to see, its blows went wild. Some robbers, seeing their leader in such parlous plight, turned away and rode off into the forest, and no amount of frantic gestures by the now headless body served to rally them. And presently, three troopers got the body amongst them and hacked it to pieces, whilst all the robbers who had not fled were likewise slain. And the folk hereabouts claim that at certain times, especially on nights of the full moon, they see Oswic's headless body, still riding about on the slopes of Aravia and brandishing a sword."

* * *

"Quite a story," said Jorian. "Does Oswic's ghost ride the ghost of his horse?"

Turonus chuckled. "None hitherto has brought up that point."

"Do you tell this tale to all your guests?"

"Oh, aye, it makes a good one to pass a long even, and primes some to tell me stories in their turn."

Jorian had been alerted by the taverner's name, the same as that of the Chancellor of Xylar at the time of Jorian's aborted execution. Cautious questioning, however, indicated that this Turonus had never even heard of his namesake, let alone admit to kinship. Still, Jorian thought it prudent to go under one of his pseudonyms, Nikko of Kortoli. He asked:

"Could one ride a horse up to the timberline, stake it out there, and walk the rest of the way? I do not anticipate being with Shenderu more than an hour or two."

Turonus frowned. "Ye could, but there's a tiger in these forests, having wandered over from the Mulvanian side. Leaving your steed tethered were a sure way of losing him."

"Then could I board my horse with you until my return?"

"Certes; 'tis usual. Now, an ye would, I'll see ye have needfuls for a call upon the Greatsoul. Many pilgrims, coming to consult the wise one, pass through here in summer, but few at this time of year. And speaking of snow, ye will need a pair of these."

Turonus stepped behind his bar and brought up two oval wooden frames on which had been stretched a netting of rawhide thongs.

"What are those?" asked Jorian.

"Snowshoes. I can rent you a pair for ten pence a day. On the trail up Aravia, ye'll need them for certain."

Jorian chaffered the man down to five pence a day. He did not altogether believe the story of the tiger, suspecting his host of making it up in order to profit from boarding the horse Fimbri. On the other hand, he could not be sure; so, lacking time to investigate the matter, he acceded to Turonus's recommendation. When Turonus also tried to sell him firewood, Jorian declined, saying: "I brought an ax and a saw to cut my own."

"Well then, belike you'd like a guide. With snow on the ground, the trail's easily lost, and ye could wander for days amongst the peaks ere finding it again. My nephew Kynoc's to be had, for he knows the lay of the land."

Further bargaining enlisted the services of Turonus's nephew, a slender, smooth-faced, small-featured youth. "How long to reach Shenderu?" asked Jorian.

"Ye must needs camp out one night, at least going up. Methinks ye'd better camp below the snow line."

When time came to go, Kynoc saw the crossbow that Jorian had strapped to the back of the pack mule. The youth asked: "Plan ye to hunt on the way, Master Nikko?"

"Maybe," said Jorian. "You'd better bring one, too."

Actually, Jorian was not interested in hunting. He wanted to get to Shenderu, resolve his problems, and hurry back to Othomae. But, having been pursued before by Xylarians intent upon dragging him back to complete their ceremony of royal succession, he thought it well to be prepared. He wore sword and dagger and a vest of light mesh mail beneath his jacket.

"Ho!" said Jorian sharply, halting. He was towing the pack mule Filoman, while Kynoc trudged ahead up the slope. The forest had begun to thin out with altitude. A light snow covered the ground between the black boles of the leafless trees. Here and there rose stands of evergreens, dark green in the light and black in the shadow.

"Eh?" said Kynoc, turning.

"Look at that!" Jorian pointed to a large paw print in the snow. "Is that the tiger your uncle spoke of?"

The youth bent down. "Aye, that's old Ardyman the Terrible. Hold the mule straitly lest it bolt. We think Ardyman has been chased from his former range by a younger cat, and that with age he's like to turn man-eater. We've tried to hunt him down in parties with hounds, but the crafty villain gives us the slip."

The mule seemed to have caught a whiff of tiger, for it jerked its head and rolled its eyes.

Since dark was falling, Jorian decided to camp here. He tethered Filoman securely, put a nosebag over its head, and got the ax and saw from his gear. He chopped down and trimmed four small dead trees, while Kynoc sawed them into billets. Jorian kept raising his head to peer into the gathering darkness for signs of the tiger.

"Best we make a goodly fire," said Kynoc.

"No doubt; but let's not burn up all the wood we've cut. We shall need some for Shenderu."

Jorian passed an uneasy night, alternately dozing and waking to listen for the grunt of a hunting tiger. Once he awoke to find Kynoc, whose turn it was to watch, asleep with his back against a tree. He angrily shook the youth awake.

"Be not so much atwitter, lowlander," drawled the youth. "The tiger won't come nigh whilst the fire burns bright; at least, not unless he starves."

"Well, for aught we know he may be starving," grumbled Jorian. "Come along; it's nearly dawn."

"Best do on your snowshoes," said Kynoc, strapping on his own. "Deep snow begins soon."

Jorian found that walking with snowshoes took practice. If one tried to walk in the normal manner, one stepped on one's own feet. Jorian did this once and sat down in the snow. He got up cursing, to see Kynoc's face agrin.

"Ye must learn to waddle, like this," said the youth, demonstrating a spraddle-legged gait.

When Jorian had mastered snowshoes, he found that the mule had turned balky, either because of the weight of the firewood, or the increasing steepness of the trail. The rest of the journey was made with Jorian hauling on the lead rope, while Kynoc beat Filoman's rump with a switch that Jorian had cut from a branch.

"Master Nikko," said Kynoc, "ye come from the lowlands and have seem more of the world than I. Tell me, is it true that down there any woman will lie down for you an ye but ask her?"

Jorian stared. His breath was becoming labored with the climb, but the spindly mountaineer youth seemed to mind the grade no more than a stroll on level ground.

When he had taken a couple of deep breaths, Jorian answered: "Some. Not all by any means."

"Tell me more about it, pray. I have never done it or seen it done. I do but hear tales from other lads, of their adventures with women and sheep and other things. Many stories I am sure are lies. So tell me: how do ye do it? How long does it take?"

When Jorian paused for a breather, he gave Kynoc a lecture on elementary sex. The youth hung on his words with an intentness that Jorian found embarrassing.

"I thank you, sir," said Kynoc, with more respect than he had hitherto shown. "My parents are dead, and my uncle and his goodwife think it a subject not to be talked on by decent folk."

The sun was well up when the two men and the mule plodded up the path to Shenderu's cave. Below, the foothills of the Lograms spread out, the taller peaks covered with snow on which the bright morning sun glittered.

They found Shenderu, bundled in shapeless brown woolens, sweeping snow from the terrace before his cave. He proved a burly, dark-skinned man of middle age, with a gray-streaked beard. Jorian said:

"Hail, reverend sir! I am Nikko of Kortoli, here on the recommendation of your friend Karadur."

"Ah, yes, dear old Karadur!" said Shenderu, in Novarian with a strong Mulvani accent. "Is that load on the mule for me?"

"Aye, save for our blankets and other personals. I seek advice."

Shenderu sat down on the rocky surface of the space he had cleared of snow. "Say on, my son."

Jorian said: "Kynoc, unload and feed Filoman. Now, Father Shenderu, my problem is this...."

The sun was halfway to noon when Jorian finished his tale. He had let his bent for storytelling run away with him; but the wise man seemed amused. Jorian finished:

"...so you see, I have tried direct assault on the palace to rescue my darling, and that failed. I tried sorcery, to no avail. What recourse remains?"

Shenderu remained sunk in thought with his eyes closed. At last he looked up, saying: "Have you tried simple bribery?"

Jorian clapped a hand to his forehead. "Good gods! I never thought of that."

Shenderu smiled. "Every large enterprise, be it a merchant company, an army, a ship, or a government, requires a multiplicity of people, organized with lines of command and a hierarchy of ranks. Wherever such a multiplicity exists, there is at least one wight open to bribes."

"How can I find a suitable bribee?"

"You have a brother who visits the palace, have you not?"

Jorian started. "Aye, but how knew you? You must know who I really am."

"I have heard much about you, Jo— What said you your nonce name was?"

"Nikko of Kortoli. For obvious reasons, neither my brother nor I wishes to disclose his kinship to me."

"I understand, Master Nikko. I know somewhat more of you than you would think. Never fear, I wag not an indiscreet tongue, as you have been known to do. My livelihood depends upon my name for reticence. Is your brother discreet?"

"Reasonably so."

"Very well. Set him to learning who is corruptible amongst the clerks and flunkeys that infest the palace. Inveterate gamblers make the best prospects, since they are usually up to their eyebrows in debt. And now perchance you'll join me in a light repast ere returning to the mundane world."

As they ate, clouds drifted athwart the sun. Kynoc said: "Master Nikko, methinks we'd best take our leave, an we'd make our return journey without camping out. Besides, it looks like rain or snow. Unless, that is, ye'd liefer ask the Greatsoul for shelter."

Jorian shook his head. "I'm hot to get back to the Golden Ibex. Let's forth! Thanks and farewell, Doctor Shenderu!"

Going down was much faster than going up. The mule was readier to move without its load of food and firewood, or perhaps it visualized the comfort of Turonus's warm stable.

While they were still above the timberline, rain began. It grew swiftly heavier; the wind rose to a howl and blew the rain into their faces. Jorian tried backing down the slope, but tripped on a rock and sat down again.

"I shall have a black-and-blue arse tomorrow," he growled as he got up.

After an hour of plodding through slush and staggering on slopes where rain made the snow slippery, they reached the shelter of the trees, as much as these leafless trunks could provide shelter. Then the rain gradually dwindled to a drizzle and ceased. They removed their snowshoes.

Kynoc sneezed. "Master Nikko, methinks we'd best halt long enough to eat a bite and dry out."

"Can we still reach the inn without an overnight stop?"

"I am sure of it, sir. By dark we shall be down to familiar country, which I know like the palm of my hand."

"Very good. Tether Filoman whilst I cut firewood, if my tinder hasn't gotten wet."

The tinder was dry, but the brushwood was not, so that it took an hour for Jorian to get a brisk fire going. He and Kynoc draped their outer clothing on nearby branches. They also wrung out their sodden blankets and hung them likewise.

Then they stood as close to the fire as they dared, turning slowly to heat all sides. The afternoon sun broke briefly through the clouds, sending golden spears of light aslant among the trees. All was quiet save for the crackle of the fire and the drip of rainwater from branches.

"I am as dry as I am likely to get," said Jorian. "Kynoc, in my bag on Filoman you will find an oil flask and a rag. Pray fetch them and help me to oil this mail shirt, ere it rust."

The youth was rubbing the mail with the oily rag when Jorian cocked his head. He said: "Didst hear someone call?"

"Aye, but so faintly methought I was hearing things."

As Kynoc finished annointing the links, the call came again, more clearly but still distant: "Oh, Jo-o-oria-a-an!"

"Halloo!" Jorian shouted, peering over the edge of the fell.

"Where are you?" came the call.

"Right here."

"Is that your fire?" The voice, vaguely familiar, came louder.

"Aye. Who are you?"

Movement among the tree trunks, down the slope, sorted itself out into a human figure scrambling up the trail. Jorian pulled on his trews, donned his damp jacket, and got his crossbow and bolts from the mule's back.

As the figure came closer, it appeared to be that of a youth in hunting gear, unarmed save for a sheath knife at his belt.

Closer yet, the figure took on a maddening familiarity that Jorian could not quite place. As it scrambled up over the lip of the fell, Jorian said: "Great Zevatas, are you the twin brother of a lady I know?"

The figure stood panting. When it got its breath, it spoke: "Nay, I'm the lady herself." Margalit swept off her forester's felt hat, so that her curly hair sprang out from her head.

"Good gods! I'm glad to see you; but what brings you hither, and in man's clothing?"

"I came to warn you. The Xylarians are on your track. 'Tis not unlikely they're already ascending the trail below us."

"How—what—how learned you this?"

"I'll tell. 'Twas Goania's wench Vanora. I gather that she besought you to take her on this journey as your leman, and you denied her?"

"Aye. So what befell?"

"The night after you left, I was dining with the old Mulvanian and with Mistress Goania and her two domestics. Vanora got drunk and had a rush of conscience. With tears and sobs she told us that, the very morn you departed, she gave a letter to the courier to Xylar, telling the government there whither you had gone. At that time, she said, so filled with hatred and rancor was she that she looked forward with glee to attending your execution and cheering with the rest as the ax fell. Now she was shamed and abashed. She wept and wailed and called on the gods to chastise her; she bemoaned her thwart nature, which forced her to do such horrid things."

"But you—how did you—"

"Someone had to warn you, and I was the only one young and active enough of our little circle. So I borrowed these garments from Rhuys's younger son, since my gowns are unsuited to riding and mountain climbing. I also borrowed Rhuys's best horse, without his knowledge I'm sorry to say, and followed your track.

"Last night I stayed at the Golden Ibex. Being weary, I retired early; but I was awakened by sounds of revelry below. This morn I arose ere daybreak. At breakfast, Turonus's daughter told me that one Judge Grallon, a Xylarian official, had come in with six attendants. These she described as tall, light-haired men of wild, barbaric aspect. That sounded like Shvenish lariat-men; so, tarrying no longer, I set ou in search of you."

"Were the Shvenites abroad when you left?"

"Nay; the maid said they were all in drunken stupor. But they'll have set forth by now, I ween."

Jorian bit his lip. "Kynoc!" he said. "Canst guide us back to the inn by another route, one that would take us around these pursuers?"

"Not with the mule, sir. This trail's the only way down for beasts, until ye come anigh the inn, where the ground's flatter. I could take you by another where ye'd need but to lower yourselves down banks by gripping the roots of trees."

"Much as I hate to leave Filoman as booty, I mislike the thought of Uthar's ax even more," said Jorian. "Put out the fire, Kynoc. I'll take my saddlebags—"

"Too late!" cried Margalit.

Cries came from down the slope, and figures appeared among the trees in the distance. Jorian recognized Judge Grallon's voice, commanding: "There they are, where you see the smoke of their fire! Spread out! Moruvikh, farther over to the right! Ingund, to the left!"

"We cannot easily lose them in the forest," said Kynoc,

"with the leaves off the trees. Would ye flee back up the trail?" The youth shook with nervousness.

"Nay; they'd catch us more easily with their ropes and nets in the open. Get your crossbow! This little fell's a good place to make a stand. The squad does not usually bear missile weapons. Watch our flanks whilst I defend our front. Margalit, help Kynoc to watch for rogues stealing upon us."

Jorian cocked his crossbow, lay prone in the leaf mold at the edge of the fell, and sighted. The movements among the trees resolved into three or four men—he could not judge their exact number—plodding up the slope. As one on the trail came into plain view, Jorian called: "Stand, varlet!"

The man, a tall, light-haired Shvenite, paused. Judge Grallon's voice boomed from back in the trees: "Go on, faintheart! He cannot hurt you!"

Jorian waited until he got a clear view of the man. He squinted along the groove of his crossbow, adjusted its angle for distance, and allowed a hair for windage. Then he squeezed the trigger.

The bow snapped; the quarrel thrummed away, rising and falling, to strike home in the Shvenite's body. Kynoc discharged his own weapon; but his bolt grazed a branch and glanced off at an angle.

The man who had been struck cried out and folded up on the ground. Grallon called: "Get down, all of you!" Thereupon the other Shvenites dropped to hands and knees, crawling forward. Most of the time they were out of sight behind dead ground.

Kynoc started to rise to recock his weapon, but Jorian barked: "Keep down!"

Plaintively Kynoc asked: "How then shall I reload?"

"Watch me," said Jorian. He rolled over on his back, put his toe in the stirrup at the muzzle of the crossbow, and pulled back on the string with both hands until it caught on the sear. Then he rolled back on his belly and put a bolt in the groove.

"I never thought of that," said Kynoc.

"You're used to shooting at deer and hares, which do not shoot back. Next time, shoot not until I tell you. We have no bolts to waste."

"Go on! Go on!" called Grallon's voice. "Creep up and surround them; then rush upon them from all sides. They cannot number more than two or three."

Jorian bellowed: "Promus, take these javelins off that way. See if you can spear one of these knaves. Clotharo, take the spare bolts off that way; try to hit one in the flank. Nors, get the covers off our shields. Physo, did you remember to sharpen our steel?"

Kynoc looked about in a bewildered way at hearing these commands addressed to nonexistent warriors. Margalit, catching on at once, lowered her voice to sound mannish, calling: "Here you are, sir. Which sword do you wish? Let me lace on your cuirass!"

The creeping Shvenites seemed to have halted their advance. Jorian whispered: "Kynoc, steal off amongst the trees on either side and tell me what you see."

"Go on!" came Judge Grallon's voice. "Keep advancing! It is all a pretence, his having an army. Get in close and rush them!"

A guttural voice spoke in the Shvenish language: "Why does he not lead his grand charge himself?" Jorian understood the words but supposed that Grallon did not.

From the trees on one side came the thud of Kynoc's arbalest, followed by a yell of pain. The young man came loping back, grinning.

"I got one!" he chortled. "Methinks I did but wound his leg; but he'll molest us no more."

"That will hold them up for a while," said Jorian. "But in a couple of hours, darkness will fall, and we shan't be able to hit the side of Mount Aravia."

"Belike we can then give them the slip," said Kynoc.

Jorian fidgeted, trying to get another clear shot. But the Shvenites hugged the hollows in the earth, offering no targets save an occasional glimpse of a buckskin-clad arse as they wormed their way forward. Jorian shot at one such target but missed.

91

At last Jorian, unwilling further to prolong the stale-mate, crawled back from his edge. "Kynoc!" he said. "I'll try a cavalry charge. Take off the rest of Filoman's load."

"How shall ye guide the beast without a bridle?"

"I'll make one." Jorian began experimenting with the lead rope, threading it through the mule's unwilling mouth and twisting it around the animal's muzzle. The mule jerked its head uneasily.

"Be it trained to riding?" asked Kynoc.

"We shall soon find out. There, that should serve to guide the beast, if he does not chew the rope through. Wilt give me a hand up?"

Since the mule had no saddle, Kynoc made a cradle of his hands, into which Jorian put one booted foot, and then he swung aboard the mule's bare back. Jorian had not ridden bareback in years and hoped his riding muscles were still hard enough to keep him on Filoman's back.

"Here goes!" he said, drawing his sword and thumping the mule's ribs with his heels.

Filoman refused to move. When Jorian whacked its rump with the flat of his sword, it shook its head and bucked. Jorian caught its mane to avoid a fall.

"Get my spurs out of the baggage," said Jorian. Margalit, again anticipating his needs, was already burrowing into his gear. Soon she had strapped the spurs to his feet.

"Here goes again," said Jorian, digging in his spurs.

The mule snorted and bounded forward, almost precipitating Jorian back over its rump. When he recovered his seat, he tried to guide the animal by his improvised bridle. But Filoman paid no heed to Jorian's rope. Instead, it ran around in a circle, bowling over Kynoc. Then it galloped off into the woods at random.

In front of it hung Jorian's blanket, which Jorian had suspended from a convenient branch to dry. The mule plunged ahead, ducking its head beneath the lower edge of the blanket. Jorian ducked, too, so as not to be swept off the mule's back by the branch. Hence he struck the blanket squarely, so that it was whisked from the branch and settled down over his head and body, completely blinding him. He yelled: "Halt! Stop! Whoa!" and pulled on the rope, to no effect.

From somewhere before him he heard a shout of terror and, in Shvenic, cries of "Oswic's ghost!" "The headless horseman!" "All is lost!" "Flee for your lives!"

Then came the sound of men running away. One tripped and fell, got up cursing, and ran on. The mule continued galloping, turning this way and that, trying to shake Jorian off. Jorian dropped the rope, caught the mane, and clung to the animal's back.

The mule stopped so suddenly that Jorian was thrown forward over its head. He landed in a patch of brush, while the blanket flew off over his head. Scratched and bruised, he scrambled up and made a flying dive to seize the mule's rope before the beast ran away.

Then he saw a curious sight. Gray-bearded Judge Grallon was kneeling on the forest floor and praying with his eyes closed. Of the Shvenish lariat-men there was no sight save a glimpse of one buckskin-clad back receding in the distance. The man limped, and Jorian guessed that he was the one Kynoc had shot in the leg, left behind by his speedier fellows. Up the trail, half a bowshot away, lay the body of the man whom Jorian had shot.

Jorian gathered up his sword, which he had dropped, and approached the justice, sword in one hand and lead rope in the other. "Get up!" he said.

Grallon opened his eyes. "King Jorian!" he cried. "Methought 'twas the true headless ghost whereof the innkeeper told us. Being too old to flee with that squad of superstitious cowards, I was confessing my sins to Imbal, expecting each instant to be my last. What would you of me? My life?"

"Not yet," said Jorian. "I need you as a hostage. Get up, pick up that blanket, and walk ahead of me. At the first untoward move, you shall be a headless ghost, too!"

Grallon grumbled: "But, Your Majesty, I do but my duty. I wish you well in every way, so long as you in turn perform your duty, which is to attend the ceremony of succession."

"Never mind that. Pick up that blanket!"

Jorian saw that the judge was looking past him with an expression of alarm. Quickly turning, Jorian saw a patch of striped orange and black among the trees. The tiger padded to where lay the Shvenite whom Jorian had shot. The cat lowered its head to sniff at the corpse, then raised it to stare at the two men on the path below. It blinked its big yellow eyes, then lowered its head again. Silently, it sank its fangs into the body.

The Shvenite gave a faint cry. But the tiger raised its head, so that the wounded man's arms and legs dangled. It walked calmly off into the forest, the man's limbs flopping where they were dragged over roots. Grallon said:

"Your Majesty is a villain, if you will excuse my saying so. Odovald was the best man of the squad, and you slew him. Were we in Xylar, you should answer for your crime!"

"Horse apples!" snorted Jorian. "I warned him to let me alone. When he would not, I defended myself. Besides, I did not slay him; the tiger did. But enough legalistics; march!"

Soon after dusk, Judge Grallon, his wrists tied by a strip of cloth cut from Jorian's blanket, stumbled up to the front door of the Golden Ibex. Behind him came Jorian, covering him with a cocked crossbow; then Margalit and Kynoc, the last leading the mule.

At Jorian's command, Kynoc went into the inn and brought out his uncle Turonus, who whistled at the sight. "What is this, Master Nikko? Some quarrel or feud? Not in my inn—"

"Never mind your inn," said Jorian. "Your other guests were after my head. Give me the reckoning, pray."

Turonus felt in the pocket of his apron and brought out a stack of thin wooden tablets threaded on a thong. He leafed through these until he came to Jorian's and presented it.

"Hers, too," said Jorian. He handed Margalit his purse, not wishing to have to juggle his weapon and the money at the same time. While Margalit counted out the money, the Shvenites appeared in the doorway.

"Your Honor!" cried one, starting to draw his sword. "What betides?"

"Back inside!" said the judge. "Quickly, ere this desperado puts a bolt through my brisket!"

Jorian smiled. "Now, your Honor, you shall come for a ride. Kynoc, saddle the judge's horse and boost him up on its back. Then saddle the lady's and mine."

Minutes later, Jorian and Margalit rode off on the road to Othomae. Jorian led the mule. The judge, gripping the mane with his bound hands, unhappily bounced on the back of his own horse, like him old and fat.

"I am in your eternal debt, Lady Margalit," said Jorian. "Why did you go to such effort and risk to save my unworthy neck?"

"I told you, I felt responsible to Estrildis for you. As it was, I did not truly save you, since the Shvenites were close upon my trail. Your own valor did that."

Jorian chuckled. "If you but knew the horror with which I felt myself borne along willy-nilly on that cursed mule, blinded by the blanket—but there, Karadur is ever at me not to let my modesty show. At least you gave me a few moments' warning. You are a splendid person. When you get a husband, you deserve the best. If I were not a devoted family man...." Feeling that his unruly tongue was about to run away with him, Jorian ceased talking and concentrated on the road ahead.

❈❈❈❈❈❈❈❈❈❈❈❈❈❈❈❈

VI

THE WATER WIFE

AFTER RIDING THROUGH THE DARK FOR HOURS, JUDGE
Grallon called: "Your Majesty, how much farther wilt drag
me? 'Twill take all the morrow to get back."

"You shan't get back," said Jorian. "I am taking you to
Othomae."

"By Imbal's iron pizzle, what for? Mean you to slay me
there?"

"Not at all, your Honor. I have a task, wherefor you are
uniquely qualified."

"Task? Art mad? What task could I possibly perform
for you?"

"Service as arbitrator in a dispute. You will receive the
standard fee and be sent back to Xylar no worse for wear."

"That is the strangest proposal I have ever heard!" exclaimed Grallon. "Why should you trust me to deliver a
just verdict, after you have treated me so wrongfully?"

"Because I knew you of old, when I was King. Will you
do it?"

Grallon hesitated. "Only if I can discharge my office
honorably, without prior conditions or constraint."

96

"That's my wish, too. I ask not that you incline to my cause because of my connection with Xylar, and even less that you incline against it because of the strong measures I have taken to protect myself."

"Very well, then," said Grallon. "Meanwhile I am half dead from bouncing on the back of this cursed beast. At least unbind me. Do you mean to camp out?"

"Nay. We shall soon reach another inn."

"And who is this young person?"

"You shall know in good time."

"At least tell me whether it be male or female."

"Not just yet. Ah, methinks I see a light through the trees! When we go in, I shall be Nikko of Kortoli, and you Master Grallon. Think not to raise an outcry of kidnapping, for we are now well within Othomaean territory. You know the love between Othomaeans and Xylarians! They'd say, give him an extra kick for me!"

At the inn, Jorian took a room for two. He offered no explanation of Margalit in her young man's garb. If anyone noticed the unmasculine bulges beneath her jacket, they forebore to comment in the presence of one so formidable-looking as Jorian.

Leaving the taverner to warm up leftovers for their supper, Jorian shepherded his two companions into the room. As he set down their baggage, Margalit took off her forester's hat, so that her curly hair sprang out.

"I know you now!" said Judge Grallon. "You are the Queen's lady-in-waiting, Margalit of Totens. I heard of your disappearance from the palace. What do you here? What of these wild tales of a scarlet demon's snatching you from the Queen's apartments?"

"Just a little sorcery gone awry," said Jorian.

"But—but that does not explain her being with you on Mount Aravia! And in men's garb, forsooth! She evanished from the palace in the month of the Eagle, and here it is almost springtime! What have you twain been up to in the meantime?"

"That's enough questions," said Jorian. "You forget you are my prisoner and not the other way round."

The judge turned to Margalit. "But you, Lady Margalit?

What do you here? Are you in some plot with this runaway king?"

Margalit began: "Why, as to that—" Then she saw that Jorian, standing behind the judge, was making motions of clapping his hand over his mouth. "You must needs ask Master Jorian," she said.

"Hah! Were this Xylar, you'd soon be behind bars as a fautor of King Jorian's felonies!"

"Felonies?" said Jorian.

"Certes! For the king to escape the doom assigned him by our divinely inspired laws were a heinous offense. Should we ever win you back to complete your part in the blasphemously interrupted ceremony, you will be scourged, ere you are beheaded, for your irreligious contumaciousness."

"Thanks for the warning," said Jorian. "I'll take good care not to be caught."

The judge clenched his fists, stamped his feet, and sputtered with righteous indignation; but so wrought up was he that no words came forth. At last he dropped his arms and dropped his shoulders, muttering: "Shameless! Shameless! You are lost to all considerations of morality!"

"Lost or not," said Jorian, "the innkeeper should have something for us to eat. Belike a full belly will help you bear my iniquities."

After supper, Jorian chivvied his companions back to the room. "Margalit," he said, "the judge shall have the bed, whilst you and I take turns sleeping beside him and watching him."

Grallon groaned. "If the word gets out that I have passed the night in bed with this young woman, my repute on the bench will be ruined, not to mention what my wife will say."

"When I said 'sleeping,' I meant just 'sleeping,'" said Jorian. "Anyway, if you keep silent about it, we will do likewise. Eh, Margalit?"

She laughed. "I have already been compromised to the point where one more scandal matters not. I promise, your Honor, to make no lascivious advances."

"Now," said Jorian, "I'll trouble your Honor for your shoes, knife, and purse."

"Aha, so Your Majesty has turned robber as well as abductor?"

"Not at all. They shall be returned to you in due course. I merely wish to make sure that, if the one of us on watch fall asleep, you do not stab us in our sleep and flee. Margalit, whilst you are on watch, sit on the judge's things."

The return to Othomae took Jorian half a day longer than had his journey to the Golden Ibex. Two companions, he found, inevitably slowed him down, the more so since one was elderly and Jorian's own horse was showing fatigue. They arrived on the afternoon of the fourth day out of the Golden Ibex, too weary to take up Jorian's business with Abacarus. Jorian did, however, hire one of Rhuys's sons to carry messages to Abacarus and to Goania and Karadur.

At dinner time, Goania and Karadur came to the Silver Dragon. Boso hulked in and gave Jorian a surly greeting. Jorian asked: "Where is Vanora?"

Goania said: "I suppose Margalit has told you of her confession. I served her notice that one more such buffoonery and she was through. She hung around for another few days. But when, by my second sight, I told her that you had escaped the lariat squad and were on your way back to Othomae, she packed up her scanty gear and vanished. Belike she thought you would slay her on your return."

"I do not kill women," said Jorian. "But I might have been tempted to stripe her backside."

Once convinced of Judge Grallon's identity, Doctor Abacarus accepted the learned jurist as arbitrator. He and Jorian drew up a stipulation of facts not in dispute and handed the sheet to Grallon. Then each set forth his argument over the debt, and each had a chance to rebut the other's statements.

When they had finished, Grallon retired to think. While

they waited, Abacarus and Jorian killed time with a game of draughts. Jorian thought himself a competent player, but the sorcerer beat him so easily that Jorian suspected magical assistance.

Grallon returned, saying: "On due consideration, I must find for Master Jorian. Doctor Abacarus, your arbitration agreement states that I collect my fee from the loser. Ten nobles, please."

Abacarus counted out the money with the expression of one who has bitten into a lemon. "Not bad pay for a morning's work," he grumbled.

"It is the going rate, sir. Your agreement also forbids either party to attempt future harassments, by dunning specters or otherwise, does it not?"

Abacarus nodded tight-lipped. Jorian saw the judge out. He said: "The first diligencia of the season leaves for Xylar on the morrow. I have reserved a place for you. Permit me to thank you for your just verdict."

"No thanks are due," grumped Grallon. "I did but call the hit as I saw it. I will confess that I was not entirely regardless of the fact that, if Abacarus clapped you in debtor's prison, our chances of getting you back to Xylar were lessened. On the other hand, the rascal richly deserved to lose. He whispered to me that, if I decided for him, he would split his takings with me."

At the inn that evening, Jorian told Margalit of the judge's impending departure. She said: "I suppose I ought to return to Xylar with him."

"Better not," said Jorian. "Remember what he said about your being an accessory to my crimes? If he got you to Xylar, he'd denounce you to the law instanter.

"He is a fanatic in his way. When I was King, he made a fine chief justice, absolutely incorruptible and fearless. You saw how he stood up to me when I held his life in my hand. But these virtues become awkward when one is on the other side of the law from him, no matter how absurd the law. And I like your head much better attached to the rest of you."

Jorian told her of his interview with Shenderu, adding:

"Know you anyone around the court susceptible to a bribe? Shenderu said gambling men were the easiest targets for golden arrows."

She frowned. "Let me think. Aha! There's a proxenary clerk, Thevatas, in charge of Estrildis's expenses. I do not know of any defalcations by him, but he is addicted to horse races. He would come to our apartment from one, volubly praising the beauty and speed of the beast he had wagered on if he had won, or berating the animal as bait for crows when he had lost."

"If I know such gentry," said Jorian, "he will have skimmed a little here and there off my darling's income to make up for his losses. We'll see what can be done with him."

"How?"

"Better that you know not. Suffice it to say that I shall depart next month. Meanwhile I must find another means of livelihood. The windmill is shut down until the spring wheat begins to come in."

When he saw the judge off, Jorian said: "Your Honor, you had better warn the Regency Council not to send any more squads of kidnappers after me. I have small influence with the Grand Duke, and he assures me that he would regard another such incursion as cause for instant war with Xylar."

This was a bluff; Jorian had never met the Grand Duke. He delayed his warning until he was sure that Judge Grallon would not have time to make inquiries to confirm or refute Jorian's story.

Grallon grunted: "I hear Your Majesty!" and climbed into the coach, which rattled away on the road to Xylar.

Jorian would like to have left for his native Ardamai right after seeing Grallon off to Xylar. But he had already missed the first diligencia of the season to Vindium, and the next would not depart for three sennights. He could not fare on horseback, because the horse Fimbri, which he had ridden to Mount Aravia, had fallen ill of some equine ailment of the lungs, rendering it useless for hard riding. Jorian was too soft-hearted to sell the beast to a

101

knacker, so he continued to maintain the animal until one day he found it dead in its stall. The knacker got the carcass at the bottom price.

Jorian decided against buying another horse for the time being. A good one would cost more than he thought he could afford. Besides, he had had enough rides over hundreds of leagues, in all weathers, to last him a lifetime.

Jorian picked up a few nobles as assistant to Tremorin, a fencing master in Othomae City. He even thought of setting himself up as a fencing master on his own; but inquiry convinced him that this was impractical. First, the city's three fencing masters would combine to suppress competition, if need be by hiring thugs to assault or kill him. Second, even if he became established, the Grand Duke would levy not only the usual tax on his earnings but also would add a surtax because he was a foreigner.

One day, Jorian saw, pinned to the bulletin board in the square, a placard reading:

MERLOIS SON OF GAUS PRESENTS

his superlative, matchless, unexcelled theatrical troupe, the Nonesuchers, performing two new plays by Pselles of Aussar, THE INNOCENT VAMPIRE and THE WRONG BEDROOM, as well as a revival of Physo's classic, THE TINSEL CROWN.

The placard bore further information about time, place, and price of admission. Jorian learned that the sheet had been tacked up by Merlois's advance man. This one told him that Merlois and his troupe would arrive that afternoon.

When Merlois lighted down from his carriage, he found Jorian awaiting him. With a yell of joy, the elderly actor and Jorian seized each other in bear hugs. Merlois whispered: "What name go you by now?"

"Nikko of Kortoli," said Jorian. "So you have your own troupe at last?"

"Aye. I wax a little old for leaping from balconies, slaying dragons, and whacking a fellow actor with a wooden sword, as my profession doth tyrannously demand. Oh, I still take small parts; I shall be the good wizard in *The Innocent Vampire*. You must attend, on pain of my august displeasure! Let me give you these passes."

"Could I beg an extra set for a companion?" asked Jorian.

"Oho, aha, so thither blows the wind! Certes; here you be. Bring a whole harem if such be your desire."

"Nay; this is merely a brotherly friendship. My heart still belongs to Estrildis, mewed up in durance vile in Xylar. I take it *The Innocent Vampire* is a horror show?"

"Aye, verily! 'Twill freeze the blood in thy veins to the consistency of cold tar, bring thy fluttersome heart to an ominous halt, and make thine eyes protrude on stalks, like unto those of the dilatory snail."

"And *The Wrong Bedroom*, I suppose, is a farce?"

"Doth the sun rise in the east? Doth the tiger devour flesh? Doth water run downhill? Indeed, sirrah, 'tis the cynosure, the acme, the epitome of farces! 'Twill shake thy belly with mirth until thy very ribs do ache, as if thou hadst been beaten by the roughhewn clubs of a regiment of Ellornian savages. I shall warn persons with weak hearts against attendance, lest they laugh themselves to death. But one thing worries me."

"And that is?"

"It is a short play, in two acts. I need something wherewith to flesh it out, lest my fickle audience deem themselves cozened. We got some bad notices on this score in Vindium."

"Hmm," said Jorian. "Since my escape from Xylar, I have betimes eked out a living as a storyteller. Thanks to the coaching you gave me in preparation for my flight, I have, I flatter myself, a fair stage presence."

Merlois clapped Jorian on the back. "Just the thing! Zevatas must have sent you in answer to my prayer, or he would have if I had thought to pray to him. You shall come on between the acts and tell one of your enthralling, fascinating, spellbinding, gripping, absorbing tales. I recall hearing some of them when I was teaching King Jorian to act."

"Am I to be paid?"

"Oh, aye, the going rate, as set by the Actor's Guild, minus your initiation fee into that cabal of graspers. When I was but a player, methought producers the world's worst tyrants, oppressors, cheats, and skinflints. Now that I am a producer, meseems that actors are the most grasping, vain, arrogant, capricious, unreasonable, untrustworthy, dissolute, and generally worthless rogues in Zevatas's world."

When the curtain fell at the end of the first act of *The Wrong Bedroom*, Jorian excused himself from Margalit and went around to the stage entrance. Presently Merlois stepped out on the stage and introduced that "celebrated, cultivated, renowned, charming, versatile, entertaining, and altogether irresistible storyteller, Nikko of Kortoli."

Jorian took a bow and said: "I shall tell the tale of a onetime king of Kortoli named Forbonian, who loved a mermaid. Know that all the kings of Kortoli since the days of Ardyman the Terrible have had names beginning with 'F.' This Forbonian was a good-to-middling king, not so brilliant as Fusinian the Fox, but far superior to that ass Forimar the Aesthete. Forbonian went about amongst the people, learning how they practiced their skills and betimes taking a hand at the plow or the loom or the hammer himself. Thus he found himself in the fishing village of Storum, helping the fishermen to haul in a net they had cast.

"The net seemed unwontedly heavy, and when with many royal grunts and heaves it was hauled ashore, it transpired that caught in its meshes was a veritable, palpable mermaid. She was not at all pleased at being snatched from her native element, and she screamed threats at the fishermen in her own language, which none understood.

"One old fisherman said: 'Your Majesty, here's a picklement. Whilst I know not her speech, I had it from my grandsire that mermaids threaten those who capture them with storms and shipwrecks, and that such calamities invariably come to pass. Let us, therefore, slay her and bury her well inland, ere she return to the sea to raise her fishy tribe against us.'

" 'That seems unduly drastic,' said the king. 'I cannot overmuch blame the sea-wench. I should be wroth if the mer-folk were to net me and draw me down into their liquid element. Let me bear her back to the palace. I will essay to turn her hostility to friendship by kind treatment.'

"So Forbonian whistled up his bodyguard. They made a litter of poles and lashed the mermaid to it, notwithstanding that she struggled and gave one guardsman a nasty bite with her needle-sharp, fish-catching teeth. Back at Kortoli City, the king commanded the guards to drop the mermaid into the royal swimming pool, which stood in a small courtyard in the palace, open to the sky. The return to the water seemed to calm her, albeit she still muttered threats and maledictions.

"That very day, Forbonian began to train the mermaid. His first task was to establish communication. This he did by offering her a reward of a small fish every time she learned a new word of Novarian. At the end of a fortnight, the mermaid actually smiled when the hour of instruction came round. She said: 'You good man, King. I love you.'

"Forbonian spent more and more time with the mermaid, to the neglect of his royal business. Since none could pronounce her name in her own tongue, Forbonian bestowed upon her the name of Lelia.

"Let me say that real mermaids are not much like the beings depicted by artists. If you imagine the lower half as the after end of a porpoise, and the upper half as a hybrid of human being and seal, you will have an idea. True, the mermaid had arms much like those of a human being, save for the webbing betwixt the fingers. Her face was more or less human, but the forehead and chin sloped smoothly back. When she swam, she cocked her head up to swim nose first, like a seal, and her head, neck, and body merged smoothly into one another. Under water, her nostrils closed tightly, like those of a seal or an otter.

"Furthermore, real mermaids do not sit on bulging buttocks on the sea rocks, combing their long hair over protrusile breasts. They have no buttocks, their breasts are small and hardly break the piscine smoothness of their shape, and their hair is but a patch of seal-like fur on their scalps. I do not think many of us would find such a creature surpassingly beautiful by human standards, although they doubtless have their own kind of beauty, just as a horse or a tiger may have.

"Natheless, a mutual sympathy sprang up between Lelia and the king, so that his greatest pleasure came to be the hours he spent beside her pool, instructing her. He took to stripping and swimming with her, claiming that she was teaching him new strokes.

"Now, King Forbonian's queen was Dionota, the daughter of the Hereditary Usurper of Govannian. Dionota was a comely female but, alas, not a sweet or companionable one. Her voice had become permanently roughened from screeching at the king, or anyone else within earshot, during her frequent tantrums. Now she became jealous of Lelia, notwithstanding Forbonian's assurances that the mermaid meant no more to him than a good horse or dog.

"At length, one day when the king was elsewhere, Dionota entered the courtyard of the pool and dumped a bucket of lye into the water. Either she mistakenly thought that the lye would instantly slay Lelia, or she did not realize how fluent in Novarian the mermaid had become, so that she would inevitably tell the king what had been done to her.

"Lelia's shrieks brought the king running, to find his mermaid writhing on the flags beside the pool, her skin blistered and inflamed. He fetched the royal physician, who used several jars of salve in coating Lelia's injured skin, and he had the pool drained and refilled.

"Lelia told Forbonian about the bucket of lye—not that she knew what lye was, but the cause and effect of her distress were plain enough. In a fury, the king went to Dionota and said: 'This is the end, you stupid bitch! Pack your gauds and get out. I am dissolving our marriage and sending you back to your father.'

"And so it was done. A month later, Forbonian got a

106

letter from the Hereditary Usurper of Govannian, saying: 'Curse it, I thought I had got rid of this peevish baggage when I palmed her off on you, but no such luck. I shall have to wed her to the Tyrant of Boaktis, whose wife has lately died.'

"Forbonian chuckled, for he knew there was bad blood between the Usurper and the Tyrant. In this way, in the guise of cementing eternal friendship, the Usurper was playing a scurvy trick on his enemy.

"Now there was no one to come between the king and his mermaid. One day he told her: 'Lelia, I truly love you. Will you marry me?'

"Lelia said: 'But Lord King, how can that be? We are of different kinds, you and I.'

" 'Oh,' quoth Forbonian, 'we shall manage. What is the use of being a king if one cannot put over things impossible to common men?'

"Forbonian went to the high priest of Zevatas to ask him to sanctify the union, but the priest recoiled in horror. So did the priests of Heryx and the other gods. At length Forbonian simply issued a royal decree, making Lelia his lawful wife.

"Then arose the problem of consummating this unconventional marriage. The doors of the courtyard had all been shut, and the only light was that from the twilit sky overhead and some candles that the king had caused to be set on the flagstones about the pool. Forbonian said to his bride:

" 'Lelia dearest, if you will hoist yourself out on the stones, we will have at it.' Lelia did not much like being out of water, claiming that the dry air made her skin itch. But she heaved herself out.

"Assured of his privacy, the king, a man of about my size, doffed his garments and set to fondle and caress Lelia. When he thought her properly receptive, he essayed to mount her; but try as he would, he could not effect an entry. At last he said: 'Devils take it, Lelia, how do they do it amongst your folk?'

" 'I am sorry,' she said, 'but my vent closes up tightly

107

when I am out of water. I cannot relax it even if I would; besides which, I find it painful to be squashed between your weight and the stones. We mer-folk always copulate in the water.'

"'Then let us try it in the water,' said the king. Both slipped into the pool. Lelia explained: 'We mer-folk approach each other side by side. We turn to face each other and, when the juncture has been made, the pair roll slowly from side to side, so that first one and then the other has its nostrils out of water. We are not fishes with gills, you know, and must needs breathe even as you do.'

"During this explanation, the cold water had robbed Forbonian of his royal rigidity; but by embracing and cosseting Lelia, he managed to restore it. When he attempted to play the part of a mer-bridegroom, however, he found that he could not time his breathing with the alternate surfacing and submersion, since Lelia expected him to stay under much longer than he could hold his breath. At every attempt, he would take a breath at the wrong time and emerge coughing and gasping, all thoughts of love banished by the urgent need to get the water out of his lungs.

"On his third try, after a long period of recuperation from the last one, Forbonian did succeed in penetrating his love. Lelia was by now in a highly excited state. In a transport of amorous passion, she seized him in her finny arms and dragged him beneath the surface. To her it was naught to submerge for a quarter-hour or more between breaths, but the poor king had no such amphibious talent.

"Soon Lelia realized that, instead of marching on to his climax, Forbonian had gone limp all over. In panic she hauled him to the surface, boosted him out on the flagstones, and heaved herself out, meanwhile shouting for help.

"The guardsmen burst in to find Lelia leaning on the prone and naked body of Forbonian, repeatedly pressing his rib cage down and releasing it. A couple of guards seized her arms, while their officer shouted: 'Drown our king, will you? Water witch, you shall beg for death ere the headsman gives the final stroke!"

"Lelia tried to explain about artificial respiration, but in her excitement she lost command of her Novarian and spoke the language of the mer-folk. They were dragging her away when the king groaned and raised himself on his elbows, gasping: 'What do you?'

"When they told him, between coughs he said: 'Release her! I risked my life by my own folly, and she saved it.'

"Forbonian issued another decree, annulling the mer-marriage. He caused Lelia to be put back into the sea, and shortly thereafter he wedded the daughter of a merchant of Kortoli City and begat heirs. But for years, they say, on moonlit nights he would go down to the sea and climb out on an old pier at Storum, and there converse with someone or something in the water below. The lesson, if you wish me to point one out, is that marriage is a chancy enough business without wantonly adding to its problems.

"And now I think the scenery has been shifted, and my old friend Merlois is ready to announce his second act. Thank you, ladies and gentlemen."

Jorian's storytelling proved so popular that Merlois kept him as an adjunct to his shows as long as the troupe played in Othomae. He insisted on taking Jorian to a costumer's shop to buy him an outfit more theatrical than his everyday jacket and trews. The costumer, Henvin, ordinarily furnished materials for the costume balls by which the gentry and nobility amused themselves. He clad Jorian in a black jacket with spangled lapels, which glittered when Jorian moved.

"Were these any wider, I could fly with them," said Jorian, looking doubtfully at the lapels.

Merlois said: "It makes you look like a proper hero of romance. How would you like a permanent post, to travel with my troupe and take acting parts as well as tell tales between acts?"

"I am flattered and grateful, but I cannot accept just now. When I get my wife back, if you still feel thus, we shall see. I am a good second-rater at several occupations, including clock-maker, farmer, carpenter, accountant, surveyor, soldier, sailor, fencing master, storyteller, poet, and I daresay actor. Which I shall finally settle into remains to be seen."

Between his storytelling for Merlois and his work at Tremorin's *salle d'armes*, Jorian managed to save some money. Hearing that the registrar at the Academy had died, he went to Doctor Gwiderius and persuaded him to give Margalit a try at the job.

"I never saw such confused records!" she told Jorian after her first day. "The old registrar must have long since discarded his trump cards. I will try to bring order out of this chaos, but 'twill be a struggle."

"How do you get on with the faculty?" asked Jorian.

"Not so different from other men. Some take me for a kind of monster, being the first woman to hold the post. As for the others—well, I can count on at least one attempted seduction a day."

"That's not surprising. You are a spectacularly attractive person."

"Thank you, Jorian. These solicitations are a compliment of sorts, even though I reject them."

In the month of the Ram, Jorian boarded the diligencia for Vindium, riding through a countryside lashed by spring rains and soon ablaze with spring flowers. At Vindium he took another coach to Kortoli. After the death of his father Evor, his brothers had moved the clock-making business from tiny Ardamai to Kortoli City. His mother remained in Ardamai, living with his sister and her family.

"Country practice is all very well, if you want to take life easily and have little ambition," said his elder brother Sillius when the greetings were over. "It is costlier here, of course, but the wealth of street trade more than makes up for it."

A couple of Sillius's children were climbing over their uncle, whom they had long heard of but never seen. "Kerin," said Jorian to his younger brother, "do you think you could get the Regency Council of Xylar to let you clean and regulate their clocks again?"

"They are about due," said Kerin, who was not only younger then Jorian but also slenderer and handsomer. "You surely provided a market for the clock-maker's skills when you reigned there, gathering all those clocks."

"It was my hobby. Some day we must try to build a clock like one I saw in the House of Learning in Iraz, powered by descending weights instead of trickling water. The engineers had not gotten it to work, but the idea looked promising."

Sillius sighed. "There you go again, Jorian! Always pushing some goose-brained newfangled idea, even though you were never able to master delicate clockwork."

"My hands may be clumsy, but it does not follow that my brain is lame," retorted Jorian. "I'll work with a large model and, when it succeeds, let you copy it in a small size, with gear wheels no larger than fish scales. Kerin, could you set out soon for Xylar, to solicit another contract to clean and repair the clocks in the palace? When I left there were twenty-six of them."

"Aye. I have bethought me of just such a venture."

"Then here is what I want you to do...."

When Jorian had explained his plans for Thevatas the proxenary clerk, Sillius said: "I wish you would not draw Kerin into your wild schemes. Some day it will come out that he is your brother, and the Xylarians will take his head in lieu of yours."

"Oh, rubbish!" said Kerin. "I have no family, as you have, and I know how to keep my mouth shut. The feast of Selindé comes up soon. Why don't we all make a holiday of it, go to Ardamai, and surprise our people there? You left seven years ago—or is it eight?—and you've never even seen your niece and nephew there. And Mother would never forgive us...."

111

VII

THE SOPHI'S TOWER

IN THE MONTH OF THE LION, JORIAN RETURNED BY COACH to Othomae. Since it was a holiday, the Feast of Narzes, Goania invited Jorian and Margalit to her house for dinner.

"You must needs take your chances on the victuals," she said. "Since Vanora disappeared, I have been trying to teach Boso to cook; but it is like teaching a horse to play the lute."

Aside from the fact that the beef was overdone, the repast did not turn out so badly as the wizardess had warned. Jorian said: "That was splendid, Boso! I see a lucrative future for you as cook in one of the big city inns, where the nobility come to eat, drink, dance, and ogle one another."

Boso dropped his usual surliness to scuff his foot on the floor. "Oh, I do try, Master Jorian," he simpered.

"But what of your plans for Estrildis?" said Goania.

"You go right to the point, my dear aunt," said Jorian. "I spent hours in Ardamai plotting with Kerin. He should be in Xylar, tending the clocks in the palace. When I get a letter saying 'The fish is hooked,' I shall set out with Karadur."

"Hai!" said Karadur. "You said not that you intended to entrain me with you, my son. I am verily too aged and fragile for another of these temerarious excursions—"

"Can't be helped," said Jorian. "Amongst other things, I shall need your help to locate that cursed crown for the bribe. It's been nearly three years since we buried it, and I am not sure I could find it by memory alone."

"But I am not capable of another long ride, in all weathers, on the back of some fractious quadruped!"

Jorian thought and said: "How if we went as a pair of Mulvanian mountebanks? You've seen these little groups, traveling about in wagons, telling fortunes and stealing farmers' chickens. I could buy a cart, which we can decorate like one of those gaudy Mulvanian vehicles. You can ride in it."

"Well, that would be—"

"Wait!" said Margalit. "I shall go, too."

"What?" cried Jorian. "This will be a rough, risky trip, my lady. Much as I esteem you, why should you—"

"Because my first duty is to my Queen, and I should be with you when you meet her again."

"I really see no good reason—"

"You will. The shock of seeing you may put her into a state where she needs my care. Besides, if you are disguised as a Mulvanian, she may not believe you to be her husband. You will need me to vouch for you."

They argued some more. But Jorian, though he thought Margalit's reasons flimsy, gave in. He was not really sorry to have her as a fellow traveler. He liked her immensely and admired her good sense and ability to cope with contingencies.

"Three would crowd one of those little carts," he said. "My sumpter mule can pull the cart, if I train him in. But I shall have to buy another horse." He looked worried. "I know not if my remaining funds will stretch so far."

"Fear not," said Goania. "I can always lend you enough to tide you over, provided you stop calling me aunt! I am no kin of yours."

"Very well, Au— Mistress Goania. It is good of you. And now, what parts shall we play in Xylar? Father Karadur can tell fortunes. I have some small skill at juggling and the sort of games of chance they play in traveling carnivals. That swindler Rudops, among the shady characters I hired to teach me their skills when I was planning escape, instructed me. And Margalit—why, 'tis plain you shall be a Mulvanian dancer!"

"But I do not know Mulvanian dances—"

"No matter. I have seen them in Mulvan, and Karadur and I can teach you."

"Think you not I am too tall to pass as a Mulvanian woman?"

"Not really; at least in Xylar, whither few Mulvanians go. The folk will have no standard of comparison."

"But stay! That is not all. A couple of years ago, a traveling troupe of Mulvanian dancers and singers passed through Xylar, and Estrildis and I attended a performance. As you might guess, they surrounded us with palace guards the whole time we were out of the palace. But the dancers, male and female, all danced bare to the waist."

"That's how they do it in Mulvan," said Jorian. "Even the dames of the highest caste go to parties thus, with designs painted on their torsos."

"I will not slither around thus indecently exposed! There was a to-do in Xylar; the priests of Imbal would have closed the show, or at least compelled the dancers to cover themselves. They were still disputing the matter in the courts when the troupe departed."

"My lady," said Jorian sternly, "you're the one who wishes to accompany us on this journey. Either prepare to dance with bare breasts or stay behind!"

She sighed. "If the priests of Imbal make trouble again, 'twill be on your head! But how shall we get skins as brown as Karadur's?"

"There's a fellow in the city, Henvin the Costumer, who sells wigs, dyes, and everything else to change one's appearance. Merlois took me to him," Jorian answered.

"Must one paint one's skin over every time one washes one's face?"

"Nay; I am told that these dyes do not begin to fade for a fortnight."

"You, my son," said Karadur, "must needs learn to wind a turban. Wait!" The Mulvanian shuffled out and returned with a long strip of white cloth. "Hold still!"

Karadur dexterously wound the cloth round and round, so that Jorian's short-cut black hair was almost hidden. Goania held up a mirror.

"I look quite the Mulvanian potentate," said Jorian. "All I need is a brown skin."

"Now," said Karadur, "let me see you do it!"

Jorian spent the next hour learning to wind the turban. The first few times, the headgear fell apart as soon as he moved, slumping into loops and folds on his shoulders. The others rolled in their seats with laughter. At last Jorian wound a turban that stayed in place even when he shook his head.

"You must also shave your countenance," said Karadur.

"What, again? But I like my whiskers!"

"In Mulvan, as you should know, only philosophers, holy men, and men of the poorest caste wear them. Moreover, you will recall that at the time of your escape from Xylar, you wore a large black mustache over a shaven chin; so the Xylarians would recognize you with that adornment."

"But a full beard like mine—"

"Ah, but recently Judge Grallon saw you with your present hirsute decoration, so it were unwise to appear thus bedight. We might encounter the judge."

Jorian sighed. "Just when I think I have achieved the acme of masculine beauty, you come along and spoil it. Margalit, think you not we should be returning innward?" He rose.

Goania said: "Better not enter the Silver Dragon with that thing on your head. We do not wish folk to know that Jorian and that great Mulvanian mystic, Doctor Humbugula, are one and the same."

"I'll do it off ere we go in. Ready, Margalit?"

* * *

Jorian bid a ceremonious farewell, bowing and practicing the gestures he had seen in Mulvan. Out they went. The night was dark and foggy, and there were no public street lamps near Goania's modest house. A lamp in the wizardess's hands, as she stood in the open door, pushed back the dark a little. When she closed the door, the darkness rushed back.

"Hold my arm, Margalit," said Jorian. "One can easily turn an ankle on these cobblestones. Damn, it's blacker than the pits of the ninth Mulvanian hell."

They felt their way slowly along. Jorian peered into the murk, thinking that he would feel very silly if they got lost on a simple walk of eight or ten blocks.

Then Jorian heard quick, soft footsteps behind him. As he started to turn, a terrific blow struck his head. The ground sprang up. Dimly he heard a shriek from Margalit.

Collecting his scattered wits, Jorian rolled over to bring his attacker into view. Against the dark overcast, he made out an even darker form swinging an ax in both hands. He thought he saw the ax rise above the form's head.

He knew he should have instantly thrown himself to the side to avoid the blow. But so weak and dazed was he that he could only blink stupidly as the ax started down.

A second form—that of Margalit, from its silhouette—gave the first one a push. He heard a low snarl of "Bitch!" and saw the attacker turn toward the woman. She sprang back to avoid a sweep of the ax, but slipped on the wet cobblestones and fell. The attacker turned back to Jorian, hoisting the ax for another blow.

Then another form loomed out of the dark. The intended blow went awry. Jorian climbed shakily to his feet to see two bulky bodies grappling, grunting, and cursing. One combatant caught the other's arm and twisted. The ax fell with a clang.

"I got him, Master Jorian!" panted Boso's grating voice. "Kill the bastard!"

Jorian felt about and gathered up the ax. For an instant he hovered about the struggling pair, peering to make sure he should not strike the wrong man. Both were stocky, burly men in rough, nondescript clothes, but in the fog-shrouded darkness he could not discern faces.

"What are you waiting for?" rasped Boso.

The direction of the voice at last told Jorian which was which. He brought the flat of the ax down hard on the head of his assailant; at the third blow, the stranger collapsed.

"Why'n't you slay him?" said Boso.

"I want to know who he is and what he's up to first," said Jorian. He turned to see how Margalit fared, but she had already regained her feet.

"Are you hurt?" Jorian asked.

"Nay, save for a bruised fundament. Who is this footpad?"

"That's what I mean to learn. Take one leg, Boso, and I will take the other. How did you arrive so opportunely?"

"I heard the lady cry out and rushed into the street," said Boso.

Halfway down the block, a golden rectangle appeared in the fog as Goania's door opened again and the wizardess stood in it with a light. Jorian and Boso hauled the body in and laid it out on Goania's floor, while she leaned over it with a lamp. The man was heavyset, with a strip of cloth covering his face below the eyes. Jorian set down the ax, an ordinary workman's tool, and jerked off the mask.

"Malgo the bailiff!" he exclaimed. "I owed him a few knocks, but wherefore should he strive to murder me?"

Goania poured a dipper of cold water on the man's face. Choking and coughing, Malgo returned to consciousness.

"We should tie him up," said Jorian. "He's a strong rascal."

"I'll see to that," said Goania. She went out and returned with a couple of lengths of rope. She spoke to these and, like tame serpents, one of them wrapped itself around Malgo's wrists and the other around his ankles.

"A couple of minor spirits, whom I have enlisted in my service," she said.

Jorian peeled off the turban. The cloth was slit in several

117

places, where the edge of the ax had penetrated, and stained crimson, where blood had seeped from a scalp wound.

"My best turban cloth!" lamented Karadur.

"I'll get you another," said Jorian. "Henvin the Costumer probably carries them. I owe it to you, since those layers of cloth saved my worthless life." He turned to Malgo, now sitting on the floor with his back to the settee, glaring. "Now then, you, speak!"

"Screw you!" snarled Malgo.

"Why did you try to kill me?"

"That's my affair."

"Oh, is it?" Jorian smiled unpleasantly. "Mistress Goania, may I trouble you for assistance in opening up this mangy scrowle? I am sure you have some ingenious methods in your magical repertory."

"Let me think," she said. "There is a small Seventh Plane demon who is madly in love with me and will do aught I ask. Naturally I cannot accede to his wishes, not wishing to be burnt to a crisp. But if I loose him on Master Malgo, he will do some interesting things, beginning with the man's private parts."

"Oh, I'll talk," growled Malgo with fear in his eyes. "I wanted to slay you because you lost me my job."

"What?" said Jorian. "I had naught to do with that! I never even knew you had been dismissed."

"Well, I was, and I know you did it, by complaining to the Grand Duke."

"You're dreaming! I have not seen the Grand Duke, nor have I complained to his officers, though the gods know I had cause to. Who told you this?"

"I won't tell."

"Goania, how about that fiery imp of yours?"

"Oh, I'll tell, I'll tell. Just let not that witch set her spooks on me. 'Twas Doctor Abacarus at the Academy. I paid him a pretty penny to divine the cause of my dismissal, and he named you."

"You wasted your money," said Jorian. "Abacarus merely sought revenge on me for besting him in a dispute over a debt."

"I can tell you why Malgo was dismissed," said Goania.

"I know the Grand Duchess Ninuis—we serve on the same committee to succor the poor—and she is a great gossip. She told me the examining magistrate caught Malgo buggering a young prisoner in his cell. For some legal reason they could not pin a criminal charge on Malgo, but they could toss him out of his post."

"There you are," said Jorian. "Now, what shall we do with this scum?"

"If it was me, I'd kill him," said Boso.

"A pious idea; but then we should have a body to dispose of. And perhaps the swine has friends, who would ask after him. I suppose he is an Othomaean citizen, but I am not."

"I'd still kill him," said Boso. "If any man tried to slay me—"

"I agree with your sentiments, friend Boso; but we must be practical. Any other suggestions?"

"We could surrender him to the law," said Karadur.

"Nay," said Goania. "Jorian has the right of it. Malgo has friends in high places, little though you might expect it. There is a nest of his kind, headed by Lord — but I will not name names. This lord has power, and doubtless his intervention set Malgo free. If we have him arrested, the legal mills will grind on forever whilst Master Malgo is out on bail to make another try."

Margalit said: "We hear a lot about the corruption in high places of Vindium; but from what I hear, 'tis just as rife here."

"True," said Goania. "The difference is that the Grand Duchy has more effective means of covering its corruption in high places."

Jorian asked: "What's the source of Lord Nameless's power? Is Gwitlac the Fat one of Malgo's brotherhood—"

"Hush!" hissed Goania, looking nervously around. "Do not say things like that within the bourne of the Grand Duchy, unless you would destroy us all! But to answer your question: nay, the Grand Duke is normal in that respect. It is purely political; this lord is one of his strongest supporters. Ninuis loathes the man, but she has not been able to turn Gwitlac against him."

"We'll forget arresting Malgo, then," said Jorian. "It were more to the point to set the law on Abacarus; Malgo is but his tool."

"Aye, but the same objections apply. Abacarus would deny the whole thing, and what were Malgo's word against his?"

Margalit asked: "Could you feed Malgo a love potion or something, so that he would do whatever Jorian commanded?"

"I fear," said Goania, "that Malgo would not make a satisfactory servant, no matter what geases we put upon him. He might be made to obey Jorian, but that would not stop him from stealing Jorian's possessions, or holding a sodomitical orgy in Jorian's room in his master's absence. If we compelled him to love Jorian, his manner of expressing his love might not meet with Jorian's approval."

"You ought to make him suffer somehow," said Boso. "It's only right. If it was me, I wouldn't be a man if I let him off free."

"True," Jorian said. "But I am less interested in revenge than in getting him out of the way. We can't have him running loose here, and Goania does not think he can be reduced to useful magical slavery. Goania, can you put a spell on him to make him obey one command from me? Implicitly?"

"Aye, within limits."

"Going to make him kill himself?" asked Boso with a grin.

"Nay, though the idea has merit."

"That would not work anyway," said Goania. "The spell cannot make him contravene his basic instincts."

"How," asked Jorian, "would it be to command him to kill Abacarus? That would be a fair turnabout."

Goania said: "Be not hasty. Abacarus is a clever rogue. If I know him, he will have taken precautions. Let me send out my second sight."

She sat still, breathing deeply with her eyes closed. At last she said: "It is as I thought. He has set up a barrier that will dissolve your command when Malgo passes through it. Abacarus will then aim Malgo back at you, as in a game of paddle ball."

"Bouncing Malgo back and forth at each other could become tedious," said Jorian. He thought a moment. "I have something equally useful. Goania, how long will such a command obtain?"

"One to three months, depending on many factors."

"Then pray put it on him."

"Very well. The rest of you, leave me alone with Malgo. I will call when I have finished."

They trooped out to the kitchen. From the living room came sounds of chants and incantations in Goania's voice, and then a harsh, crackling voice that was neither Goania's nor Malgo's. Jorian killed time by telling a story. "I am sure," he said, "you have heard some of my tales of King Forimar the Aesthete. He nearly ruined Kortoli by neglecting statecraft to pursue the arts, such as music, painting, and verse, in all of which he made signal contributions.

"Then Kortoli was overrun by the armies of Aussar under Doubri the Faultless, a fanatical priest who wished to foist on other nations the puritanical austerity he had imposed upon his own land. The siege of Kortoli City was broken by the return of the naval squadron under Forimar's brother Fusonio.

"Forimar had sent Fusonio to Salimor in the Far East, ostensibly to establish trade relations, but actually to get rid of his brother, whose carping at Forimar's extravagance and neglect of public affairs vexed the king. But as the price for saving Kortoli, Fusonio forced his brother to abdicate in his favor.

"Anon, Fusonio thwarted a conspiracy by his brother to regain the throne. To prevent further attempts, Fusonio sent the ex-king to distant Salimor as ambassador. Fusonio would normally have dispatched his brother on a warship. But he had heard that the barbarians of Shven were assembling a fleet in the Bay of Norli to ravage the Novarian coasts. So he felt he had to keep the fleet at home.

"The conveyance of Forimar he trusted to a privateer, Captain Joelid, with orders to take Forimar to Salimor. Joelid bore letters of marque from Fusonio; but since Kortoli was then at peace, he was compelled to fill the rôle of peaceful trader.

"Fusonio sent a bodyguard of ten soldiers to act as Forimar's escort and, moreover, to see that he did not slip away at some intermediate port. The soldiers were young single men who had volunteered because they had heard tales of the beauty and availability of the Salimorese girls, who went about clad like those Mulvanian dancers whom Margalit saw. Fusonio also gave the officer of this detachment, Lieutenant Locrinus, a letter to the Sophi, asking that potentate to hold Forimar in genteel confinement all his life.

"So off went Captain Joelid, and off with him went Lieutenant Locrinus and the former King Forimar. Unable to find an adequate cargo in Kortoli, Joelid dropped down the coast to Vindium.

"At Vindium, Lieutenant Locrinus saw to it that the ex-king had no chance to slip ashore and escape. But he had no authority over Captain Joelid, who went ashore on his own business. After an unsuccessful day of cargo seeking, the privateer sought a tavern, where he fell in with a fellow sea captain from Salimor, one Dimbakan.

"Now, in visiting merchants and warehouses, Captain Joelid had heard of a deal very profitable to a skipper who could take immediate advantage of it. It involved a triangular trade amongst Vindium, Janareth, and Tarxia. The thought of these profits made Joelid's mouth water; but he could not sail to Janareth, to Tarxia, and back to Vindium and also carry Forimar to Salimor.

"So, when both Joelid and Dimbakan were well plied with the liquors of Vindium, they struck a deal. Joelid would turn over Forimar and his escort to Dimbakan, who was to leave for home in a few days. He would pay Dimbakan a part of the fee that Fusonio had paid him to take his brother to Salimor. He opened by offering one tenth; but Dimbakan, no stranger to chaffering, laughed in his face. After much haggling, they settled on two-thirds of the fee for Dimbakan.

"Next day, Joelid told Forimar and his men that they were going to Salimor, not on Joelid's privateering vessel, but on Dimbakan's ship, the *Itunkar*. Lieutenant Locrinus vehemently objected. But Joelid said he could make his choice: go ashore, sail with the *Itunkar*, or remain on Joelid's ship, about to leave for Janareth and Tarxia.

"As a privateer, Joelid carried a large crew for the size of his ship. These seemed a hard-bitten lot of rogues, who could easily turn to piracy if lawful occupations failed them. Lacking the force to overawe Captain Joelid, Locrinus grudgingly accepted the new plan. He and his men marched ashore, surrounding Forimar, and adown the waterfront until they came to the *Itunkar*. Two days later, Captain Dimbakan sailed.

"Forimar found himself aboard a long, narrow vessel, with outriggers to keep it upright in all weathers and two lugsails of curious shape. The voyage took a good part of a year, and Forimar was happy to disembark at the capital, Kwatna. He had learned enough of the language to get along with the Salimorese and now dressed as they did, in a simple length of cloth wrapped skirtwise about his loins.

"Since Fusonio's departure from Salimor, the Sophi who had reigned at that time had died and been succeeded by his son Mynang. The new Sophi received Forimar graciously and showed a lively interest in Novarian customs and technics.

"Forimar made a serious effort to discharge the office of ambassador in a creditable way. But he soon became moody and discontented, because there was little for him to do. Kortoli and Salimor were too far asunder to be concerned with each other's military alliances and adventures, and trading ships, selling metalware and glassware and buying tea and spices, arrived from Novaria only at intervals of months.

"So Forimar returned to his old love, art. He studied the Salimorian arts of painting, sculpture, and music. He was especially captivated by the Salimorian dance. A dancer of the royal troupe caught his eye, and he divined that neither was she indifferent to his regard. He persuaded the dancing master to present the girl, Wakti, to him. When he hesitantly said something about seeing her alone later, she replied:

"'Oh, that is no matter, my lord. I shall come to your house tonight.' Sure enough, when Forimar returned to his bedchamber after supper, he found a nude Wakti smiling invitingly.

"Although nearly forty, Forimar had never bedded a woman in his life. When he hesitated, Wakti asked him what was the matter. He confessed to being a complete tyro at love, whereupon she was convulsed with laughter, as if it were the funniest thing she had ever heard. But she said: 'That is no matter, dear Ambassador Porimar.' For so the Salimorians called him, having no F in their language. 'Come hither and I will show you how.'

"Wakti's laughter had caused Forimar to lose some of his readiness; but Wakti revived it. Afterward Forimar said: 'Great Zevatas, what have I been missing all this time! But tell me, Wakti darling, what would happen if you should conceive?'

"'Oh,' she said, 'that is no matter. We have an herb to prevent that. Now sleep for a while, and we will at it again.'

"So Forimar and Wakti became official lovers, a state on which all the Salimorese, from the Sophi down, smiled benignly. Forimar was deliriously happy. But since he could not make love to Wakti all the time, and his official duties were negligible, he took more intense interest in the Salimorian arts.

"In Kortoli he had dabbled in architecture, bankrupting the nation by building costly temples and other structures. To Mynang he suggested erecting a lighthouse like that of Iraz, of which he had heard and seen pictures, but even taller and more splendid. The Sophi, spellbound by Forimar's exotic ideas, asked Forimar to draw up a plan.

"Forimar did so, and Mynang commanded his ministers to assemble workmen and materials forthwith. He also ordained a special tax to pay for this enterprise. This tax caused much grumbling amongst the common folk, on whom it bore heavily. But Forimar, in an ecstasy of watching his tower go up day by day and at night practicing Salimorian dances with Wakti in both the vertical and the horizontal positions, knew naught of this.

"Months passed and the tower, in a square on the waterfront, soared into the heavens. So impatient was the Sophi to see it that he caused the workmen to be speeded with whips. A little over a year after the laying of the first stone, the tower was complete but for the interior furnishings. Mynang decreed a holiday for the dedication of his tower.

"A platform was erected before the tower, whence the Sophi would make a speech. The square was decorated with flowers and colored cloth. Forimar took his place in the parade behind Mynang, who was borne in a gilded litter. The band stepped out, tooting and tweedling and banging. After them came the royal guard, and then the litter.

"The procession was approaching the square of the tower, where thousands of Salimorese had already assembled, when the earth gave a slight quiver. Forimar had been so busy with his arts and with making love to Wakti that he had never learned that Salimor was a land of frequent earthquakes. Most dwelling houses were therefore low, flimsy affairs of bamboo and palm-frond matting, which would whip back and forth when shaken but remain largely intact. A few of the nobility and the Sophi, only, dwelt in buildings of masonry.

"The earth lurched again, and the tower groaned and swayed. At once, the thousands in the square began to run away in all directions. The first fugitives who raced up the street on which the parade was marching collided with the band and swept the bandsmen along with them.

"Then came the main shock. The tower groaned louder and swayed wider. Then it crumbled into thousands of separate stones, pouring down from its height like drops in a waterfall, to strike the earth with a roar heard leagues away, smashing and rebounding and shaking the city of

Kwatna almost as severely as the earthquake itself. Soon there was naught left of the tower but a huge pile of broken masonry, half hidden in a vast cloud of dust.

"Thanks to the warning shocks, the square had been pretty well cleared of spectators. Natheless, several score were killed, some by rebounding stones and some trampled to death in the rush. Many more suffered lesser injuries. Some other houses in Kwatna, including part of the palace, were shaken down with loss of life and property.

"The crowd that rushed through the street of the parade had knocked down Mynang's litter bearers, so that the Sophi was thrown out on the street. He tried to restore order, but none heeded him. A rumor ran through the crowds, that Sophi Mynang had displeased the gods and thus brought about the earthquake. Some blamed the Sophi, while others blamed his fiendish foreign crony, meaning Forimar. Mynang was recognized as he tried to get back to the palace. A mob, incited by a holy man, set upon him and tore him to pieces.

"Forimar might have suffered a similar fate, but amid the swirling crowds of Salimorese, screaming and foaming with excitement, a brown hand seized his wrist. 'Come quickly!' said a familiar voice, and Wakti dragged him through a doorway. He found himself in the house of friends of Wakti, who let her take him to a back room and hide him.

"Some Salimorese were giving thought to who should succeed Mynang in power. The late Sophi's eldest son was a boy by a concubine, six years old; the eldest by a legitimate wife was four. (The Salimorese did not allow the rule of women.) Each child had partisans, and for a day it looked as if the succession would be settled by civil war.

"Then Wakti reported to Forimar that a new leader had arisen. This was none other than the Captain Dimbakan who had brought Forimar thither from Vindium. Dimbakan harangued the crowds on the form of government he had observed in Vindium, namely a republic, with the chief officers elected at fixed intervals by the people, and no hereditary ranks of nobility. This idea was new to the

Salimorese, but they took to it with enthusiasm. Dimbakan promised that, once in power, he would forthwith hold an election to decide whether to abolish the monarchy and whom to choose to run the state.

"In a few days, Dimbakan proclaimed himself regent in the royal palace. Mynang's sons had disappeared; whether slain or smuggled away, Forimar never learned. As time passed, people asked Dimbakan when he would hold that promised election; but he always had some plausible reason for not staging it just yet. Eventually he announced that, albeit reluctantly, he would yield to the unanimous wish of the people and declare himself the new Sophi. As to how unanimous this popular desire was, we have only Dimbakan's words as reported by Forimar.

"On a visit to the hidden Forimar, Wakti said: 'My love, since the royal dance troupe has been disbanded, and you can no longer make me generous gifts, I have decided to marry.'

"Forimar said: 'Do you mean to marry me? Oh, joy! Let us be about it instanter!'

" 'What!' cried Wakti, 'Me wed you, a fugitive foreigner? Good gods, what an idea! Nay; I have a good man picked out, a journeyman coppersmith. As for you, you had better take the first ship back to your own land, ere some fanatic recognize you.'

" 'But you said you loved me!' bleated Forimar.

" 'True; so I do. But that is no matter. What has love to do with marriage?'

" 'Back in Novaria, they are supposed to go together,' quoth he.

" 'What a barbarous land!' she said. 'Here marriage is the forming of family alliances, the pooling of resources, and the building up of a stable, self-supporting family unit. Such considerations form a much firmer base for happy longtime cohabitation than mere love.'

" 'You make marriage sound like a sordid commercial deal!' he said.

" 'And why not?' she retorted. 'To eat regularly is the most important thing in life—even more so than love,

since one can live without love but not without eating—
and a well-matched pair can eat better together than
separately.

" 'Now, pack your gear, for a ship leaves on the morrow
for Vindium. I will fetch a disguise, so you can pass safely
through the streets.'

"And so it was done. Some years later, King Fusonio
visited Vindium. As usual, he sought a tavern wherein to
mingle incognito with the common folk. In this tavern,
he found himself seated near a group of fisherman, who
could easily be identified by their smell. One slender,
middle-aged fellow, with a graying beard, looked familiar.
At length this nagging half-memory so irked Fusonio that
he went to the other table and touched the man on the
shoulder, saying: 'Your pardon, my friend, but do I not
know you?'

"The man looked up, replying: 'I am Porimar of Kortoli,
a fisherman in the crew of Captain—oh!' the man stared
wide-eyed. 'I believe you do know me, and I also know
you. Let us go where we can talk freely.'

"They found a secluded corner, and Forimar (or Porimar,
as he now called himself) related his adventures. Fusonio
brought Forimar up to date on events in Kortoli. The
brothers were warily friendly. The king said: 'How do you
like your present trade?'

"Forimar shrugged. 'Not bad. There is as much art, I
find, in tracking a school of fish and managing a net as
there is in painting a portrait or cobbling together a verse.'

" 'Is there aught you would like me to do for you—
short of letting you back into Kortoli, that is?'

" 'Aye; give me the money to buy my own fishing smack
and hire a crew.'

" 'You shall have it,' said Fusonio, and so it was done.
And sometimes, when affairs of state were more than
usually vexatious, King Fusonio wondered if, perhaps, his
brother did not have the better lot of the twain. But when
he thought of the hardships and hazards of a fisherman's
life, he put aside such thoughts as sentimental
romanticism. And he resolved to get such satisfaction as
he could out of the rôle to which the gods had called him."

128

* * *

When Goania called, they came back to find Malgo standing blank-faced. The magical cords that had bound him now dangled harmlessly from the fist of the wizardess.

"Give your command, Jorian," said Goania. "Take not too long about it."

"Malgo!" said Jorian. "Wilt obey my command?"

"Aye, sir," growled Malgo.

"Then you shall leave Othomae City forthwith, travel east to Vindium, and take ship as a deckhand for the Kuromon Empire, or the Gwoling Islands, or Salimor, on whatever ship thither bound has a berth open. Do you understand?"

"Aye, sir. Can I stop back to my room to get supplies for the journey?"

"Aye, but without needless delays. Now go!"

Like a walking corpse, Malgo shambled out the door and into the night. Jorian said: "By the time the command loses power, he'll be well on his way to the Far East. Once aboard ship, 'twill avail him naught to change his mind. If he survive the voyage, he could not get back in a year, by which time I hope to be elsewhere."

"Can I dress your wound?" said Goania.

"Nay, it is but a scratch. Betwixt my thick skull and Doctor Karadur's best turban, I have nought worse than a slight headache. And thanks for saving my life, Boso."

Boso scuffed his shoe. "Oh, that was nought. You once saved mine, when we fell into Lake Volkina. Besides, you said you liked my cooking."

On the way back to the inn for the second time, Jorian told Margalit: "It is strange. I've fought with Boso thrice—not mere words, but twice with fists and once with swords. It started when he learned I was the son of the man who built Othomae's chiming municipal water clock, thus ending his job as the city's gong ringer.

"Either of us might have killed the other, for he has the thews of an ox. I thought he hated me. At the same time, I did drag him out of that lake when the Goblin Tower fell; and now he saves me from being chopped up like kindling."

Limping from her fall, Margalit said: "I once read in the *Aphorisms* of Achaemo that one should treat every friend as if he might some day become an enemy, and every foe as if he might some day become a friend."

Jorian grinned in the darkness. "Good worldly advice. But I don't think I could imagine you as my enemy, Margalit."

VIII

THE
MARSHES OF MORU

IN THE MONTH OF THE DRAGON, JORIAN RECEIVED AN UN-
signed letter, in Kerin's hand, reading: THE FISH HAS SWAL-
LOWED THE HOOK. As soon as they could gather their gear,
Jorian, Karadur, and Margalit set out. Karadur and the girl,
the latter in the masculine attire she had worn to Mount
Aravia, rode in a cart with a canvas top and two large
wheels, drawn by Filoman the mule. Jorian had spent many
weary days in training the balky animal to obey the reins
and was not altogether satisfied with the results.

Jorian himself rode a new horse, Cadwil, of better qual-
ity than the late Fimbri. When a storm blew up, Jorian
crowded into the cart and led the horse behind the vehicle.

Short of the Xylarian border, Jorian took a side road that
led southwesterly through the forest, clad in the dense
green foliage of late summer, toward the Marshes of Moru.
When the road petered out to a mere track, he halted,
tethered the animals, and left Margalit in charge. He also
left her his crossbow with instructions for its use. He was
pleased to find that she, unlike most women, was strong
enough to cock it.

Jorian and Karadur set out afoot. They followed a copy

of a map from the Grand Ducal archives and Jorian's memory of the country from his flight through it nearly three years before. Flies buzzed round their heads; Jorian slapped one that bit him in the neck. The woods resounded with the metallic song of cicadas.

At the time of Jorian's previous visit to this area, Rhithos the Smith had laid a confusion spell on the forest around his house. He did this as a favor to the Silvans, the aboriginal inhabitants, to keep hunters and woodcutters out of their woods. In return, the Silvans furnished Rhithos and Vanora, who was then his slave, with food. But when Rhithos had tried to kill Jorian in order to put a spell on a magical sword he was making, Jorian killed him instead. So the spell was broken.

They had been walking the trail for an hour, going slowly because of Karadur's age, when Jorian jerked his head back as something whispered past him. The sound ended in a sharp *tick*. Jorian saw a dart sticking in a tree beside the trail; he pulled it out. The point had been smeared with some sticky stuff.

"That must be the doing of the Silvans," said the Mulvanian. "It is doubtless poisoned."

"I thought they dwelt leagues farther east, in the vicinage of Rhithos's house?"

"Nay, they range widely through the forest belt north of the Lograms."

"But why should they shoot at me?"

"You slew their ally the smith. We had better get back to the wagon—"

Another whisper, and another dart struck another tree, this time behind them.

"Get down!" said Jorian, throwing himself flat on the trail. "Are they warning us, or are they merely bad shots?"

"I know not," said Karadur, lowering himself more slowly.

Jorian had already started to crawl back along the trail. Another dart struck his leather jacket; he snatched it out.

"They seek to slay us, forsooth!" he said. "There goes one of the losels!" A small, hairy, naked form with pointed ears and a tail flitted among the trees. "And me without my trusty crossbow! Canst work a spell to get us out of this?"

"If they would stop shooting blowguns at us, I could effect another confusion spell. It is a simple magical operation."

"O Silvans!" roared Jorian, rising on his elbows. "We are friends! Come out and let us talk!" He ducked as another dart whizzed past.

"Crawl faster!" he growled, wriggling along the trail past his companion.

"I cannot keep up with you!" panted Karadur.

"If I could get close enough to seize one.... Look you," Jorian whispered. "I'll pretend to be hit and dying. Do you likewise."

A dart flew at Jorian's face, but a twig deflected it at the last instant. "*Ai!*" screamed Jorian, thrashing about as if in his death throes. Behind him, Karadur made similar noises and motions. Then both lay still.

After what seemed a long wait, a rustle in the greenery announced the forest folk. Three appeared on the path, with blowguns made from canes. When they stepped closer, Jorian bounded to his feet and threw himself on the nearest one. Since the little fellow was only waist-high to Jorian, he was easily overcome.

The other two leaped back, squeaking in their own tongue. As they raised their blowguns, Jorian put the blade of his knife against the captive's neck.

"Don't shoot, if you want your friend alive!" he shouted.

Whether or not they understood the words, the two hesitated. Karadur came up behind Jorian and spoke in the twittering tongue of the Silvans, who answered. Then they lowered their weapons.

"What say they?" asked Jorian.

"They say they shoot all 'big folk' who trespass here. Since their friend the smith was slain, their woods are overrun with our kind."

"Tell them you will put another confusion spell if they will leave us alone."

"I was about to do so." Karadur and the Silvans conferred further.

The Mulvanian gathered twigs and started a small fire on the trail. From one of the many internal compartments of his wallet he took a pinch of powder and sprinkled it on the blaze, intoning words. The vapors made Jorian, holding his captive, sneeze.

"They say," said Karadur, "that you may release their fellow now without fear."

"I know not how far to trust these creatures."

"Oh, I am sure—"

"Aye, I have accepted your assurances to my sorrow ere this. What's their most binding oath?"

"By Thio's soul, I believe."

"Very well, tell them to swear peace with us by Thio's soul. I must release this fellow sooner or later, since I cannot dig for the crown and hold him hostage at the same time."

More twittering, and Jorian released his captive. The three Silvans faded into the vegetation. Jorian asked:

"How did you come to know so much about them?"

"I had to pass examinations in those subjects when studying wizardry at Trimandilam."

"If you knew their language, why didn't you speak to them sooner?"

"I was too frightened and out of breath."

They plodded on. Jorian sweated, swatted flies, and cast anxious looks through the aisles of the greenwood. The day wore on.

In the afternoon, they came out on the shore of a branch of the Marshes of Moru. One of the small crocodiles of the marsh slipped into the water, sending ripples out across the still, black mere, over which glittering, glassy dragonflies hovered and darted.

"This is odd," said Jorian, frowning at his map. "It looks like the middle finger of the north branch of Kadvan's Marsh. But we should be much farther south, around here," He pointed. "I thought I knew this country like the palm— great Zevatas! I know what's the matter! Your confusion spell has confused me, too!"

Karadur spread his hands. "What expected you, my son? I had no means of immunizing you from its effects."

"Does it affect you, also?"

"Not really, since I never did learn my way about this lieu so well as you did when you were King; so I have little knowledge to be twisted by the spell."

Jorian shrugged. "Then there is naught for it but to keep on trying. Come on!"

He started off on a vast circumambulation of the marshes, plowing through thickets of shrubbery and sinking into boggy patches. Karadur's fatigue forced them to stop to rest more and more often. Time and again, Jorian would set his course by the sun and start off in what he meant as a straight line, only to find soon after that he had somehow gotten turned around and was heading in the opposite direction. At sunset they were still struggling.

"I thought we should be back at the cart with the crown by now," grumbled Jorian. "I can testify that this spell of yours, at least, works fine. Had I known, I should have brought food and blankets. No use blundering on without light to see our way."

"Must we spend a night on the ground?" asked Karadur.

"So it seems. Let's hope that tiger I saw at Mount Aravia wander not down this way. 'Twere not an impossible distance for it."

Jorian built a small fire and spent an uncomfortable night, sleeping in snatches with his back to a tree and wondering whether the sounds he heard were those of some prowling predator or the rumbling of his empty stomach. Karadur seemed to manage better, settling into a cross-legged position, putting himself into a mystical trance, and awakening with dawn apparently none the worse.

They plodded on through the morning, as the cool of the night gave way to the steamy heat of midday. At last Jorian said: "We should be near our goal. The lay of this land looks familiar, unless your spell has addled what memory I have. Have you a short-range divination spell that will tell us where lies the crown?"

"Nay; that is Goania's specialty. Let me see; we buried the bauble beneath a log, did we not?"

135

"Aye. Younder lies a log; could that be the one?"

It was not; nor were the next six logs they investigated. Jorian said: "I shall have nightmares of digging under one fallen trunk after another through all eternity—ah, that one looks familiar!"

A few minutes later, Jorian gave a whoop as they dragged out a mass of rotted rags wrapped around a heavy object. The rags were the remains of the clothing from which Jorian had changed when he made a rendezvous with Karadur here on his flight from Xylar. Inside the tatters, bright and gleaming, was the crown of Xylar.

Jorian held it up to admire the glitter of the morning sun on the jewels around the rim, which flashed scarlet and azure and green. "At least, 'tis some satisfaction to have guessed right for once.... What's that?"

A sound of a heavy body moving came to his ears. He sprang to his feet, peering about. The swish of displaced branches and the thud of heavy footfalls came closer. Jorian cried:

"It's a Paaluan dragon! Up a tree, and yarely!"

Through the brush came a monstrous lizard, over thirty cubits long. Jorian sprang to the nearest large tree, an old silver-gray beech, with enough low branches for easy climbing. As he swarmed up the trunk, he turned to see how his companion fared.

Instead of climbing a tree, Karadur had loosed the rope from around his waist and laid it in a coil before him. He was chanting a spell over it. The upper end of the rope reared up, like the head of an angry cobra. As it rose to man-height, Karadur seized the tip in both hands and wrapped his scrawny legs around it lower down. The rope continued to rise until it almost stood on its tip, raising the wizard three fathoms above the ground.

The dragon came briskly to the foot of the tree that Jorian had climbed. It placed its foreclaws against the trunk and reared up, maneuvering its head among the branches and shooting out a long forked tongue. Jorian climbed higher to keep out of its reach.

The dragon backed down the trunk and turned its attention to Karadur, bunched at the top of his rope. It cocked

136

its head to one side and then to the other; it approached the rope and gingerly touched it with the tip of its tongue.

Jorian foresaw that even its small reptilian brain might have the wit to seize the rope in its fanged jaws and shake Karadur off his precarious perch. Without stopping to ponder, Jorian descended with reckless speed, ran to where the lizard was still scrutinizing the rope, and drew his sword as he ran. He aimed a cut at the dragon's tail, opening a small gash in the thick, scaly hide.

With a hoarse bellow, the dragon swung its ponderous head about to see what had stung it. Prepared for this, Jorian sheathed his sword and ran, the dragon lumbering after.

Jorian did not run so fast as he could have, knowing that if he tripped and fell, the dragon might gobble him up before he regained his feet. So he ran cautiously, watching for roots and fallen branches. Behind him came the dragon. From the sounds it made, Jorian thought it was gaining; but he held to his course.

Jorian ran and ran. His heart pounded and his breath came in gasps. At least the sounds of pursuit seemed to be getting no closer.

Then, despite his care, he put his foot into a hole in the turf, masked by dead leaves, and fell sprawling. He scrambled up, expecting the fanged jaws to slam shut on him. A glance showed him still several fathoms ahead of his pursuer. He ran on.

When his laboring lungs seemed ready to burst, Jorian became aware that the dragon, too, had slowed. He risked a glance back. The monster was still coming, but more and more slowly, like a clockwork toy running down.

Jorian slackened his own pace, taking care not to gain so much on the dragon as to lose sight of it altogether. A savant in Iraz had explained that cold-blooded organisms like lizards had less efficient hearts than birds and mammals and hence could not sustain such strenuous efforts so long. And so it had proved.

The dragon stopped altogether, lowering its huge barrel to the forest floor and lying still, save for the movements of its tongue and rib cage. Breathing great gulps of air,

Jorian watched from a distance. After a while the lizard rose to its stumpy legs and ambled off. Jorian feared it might head back toward Karadur; but instead it set out at right angles to its former direction. When it was out of sight and hearing, Jorian returned to the place where he had buried the crown.

Karadur still clung to his perch. "Is it safe to come down?" he quavered.

"Aye, at least for the moment. Didn't you realize it could seize your rope in its jaws and jerk you back to earth?"

"Oh, I thought of that. But whereas I find tree climbing impossible at my age, and we had no ladders as in the Grand Duke's park, I knew the rope would carry me up on the strength of the spell." Karadur slid to the ground. At his command, the rope fell in a limp heap at his feet. He picked it up and wound it round and round his waist. "My thanks for saving my life at the risk of your own. Whatever your faults, my son, you are a true hero."

"Oh, rubbish!" said Jorian, looking embarrassed. "Had I stopped to think, I should have been too fearful to do aught."

"Jorian!" said Karadur sternly. "What have I told you about deprecating yourself?"

"Sorry. I haven't run so hard since Estrildis's father chased me with a scythe, the first time I came over to his farmstead to spark his daughter." Jorian picked up the crown. "I feared lest the dragon swallow this. Then I should have had to slay the beast, cut it open, and dig out the crown, and I have no idea of how to do that. Let's be off, ere another come along."

"I saw none when I met you in Moru before. Whence come they?"

"That was a dragon of Paalua, from across the Western Ocean. The Paaluans used to raid the coasts of other lands to seize the folk to eat; for, albeit civilized in some ways, they retained this unneighborly habit. Several generations past, they landed on the coast of Ir, hoping to replenish their larders with Novarian captives. They brought a number of these lizards as mounts for cavalry, each dragon bearing half a dozen soldiers. When the Paaluans were crushed, some dragons found their way south to the Marshes, where they survived and bred. There have been rumors of them, but this is the first one I have seen."

By paying close heed to the map and the terrain, they finally found their way back to the wagon despite the confusion spell, which several times sent them astray. Jorian wore the crown of Xylar as the easiest way to carry it.

As they neared the glade where Jorian had left the cart, the sound of voices jerked him alert. He stole forward, motioning Karadur to keep behind him and be quiet.

As the cart came into view, Jorian saw figures moving. Coming closer, he perceived that they comprised two raggedly-clad men holding a struggling Margalit by the arms. A third was pulling things out of the cart; only his lower half could be seen. The horse and the mule placidly grazed.

Jorian slipped behind a tree as he eased his sword out of its scabbard, lest a flash of sunlight on the steel alert the brigands. Behind him, Karadur whispered an incantation.

Jorian gathered his legs beneath him and hurled himself toward the cart in a swift, silent charge. He had covered half the distance when a robber saw him and shouted: "Ho! Aldol, beware!"

The third robber, who was stripping the cart, whirled around. He was smaller than Jorian but lithe and quick. Before Jorian, his sword extended before him, could get home, Aldol had drawn his own sword, a double-curved hunting falchion.

Going too fast to stop to fence, Jorian bore in. His point plunged into Aldol's chest halfway to the hilt. At the same time, the robber brought his short sword down on Jorian's head in an overhand cut. The blade struck the crown of Xylar with a clank.

A little staggered, Jorian tried to withdraw his own blade, but it seemed to have become wedged in Aldol's spine. As

Jorian pulled, the man struck again, forehand at the side of Jorian's head. Jorian threw up his left arm. He felt the blade bite through leather and cloth into the flesh. Then Aldol sagged as his knees gave way, dragging Jorian's sword down with him.

The robbers holding Margalit released her to reach for their weapons. Still trying to free his sword, Jorian thought: this is the end; they will make ground steak of me ere I can get my hanger free.

But to Jorian's surprise, a look of terror flickered in the surviving robbers' faces, even as they drew. Instead of attacking, the pair turned and ran down the track toward the main road until lost to sight.

Jorian got his sword loose at last. The robber he had skewered moved and groaned. Jorian put his point over the man's heart and, with a vigorous thrust, quieted him.

"Jorian!" cried Margalit, throwing her arms around him. "You came just in time! They were boasting of how often they would rape me ere cutting my throat."

"Take care; you'll get yourself bloody."

"Art wounded?"

"Just a scratch. What befell?"

He peeled off his jacket and shirt. Aldol's falchion had been stopped by the ulna, but there was a freshly bleeding cut on his forearm, a finger's breadth long. As Margalit washed and bandaged the wound, she told her tale:

"I was washing my face in the stream, when these stinkards pounced upon me. The crossbow was in the wain, so I had no chance to use it. Methinks I gave one a black eye." She glanced down and saw that her shirt had been widely torn open. She pulled the edges together. "What was that I saw, as you rushed upon the chief robber? It looked like three or four Jorians, all running toward us with bared blades and all wearing golden crowns. 'Twas a daunting sight."

"Just a little illusion spell," said Karadur. "It sufficed to put the other twain to flight. Lady Margalit, if you keep much company with Jorian, one thing is sure: you will never suffer boredom. Life in his vicinage is one dire endangerment after another."

"I know not why," said Jorian in plaintive tones. "I am a peaceable man, who asks for nought but to be suffered to make an honest living."

"Perhaps," said Karadur, "you were born on the day sacred to your Novarian war god—what is his name?"

"Heryx; but I was not born on his feast day." Jorian took off the crown, in which Aldol's sword had made a deep nick. "This thing saved my brainpan, just as your turban did. I do not think the cleft will much impair its value."

Margalit exclaimed over the crown's beauty, saying: "Jorian, are you sure you wish to give it up to get your Estrildis back?"

"Of course I'm sure!" snorted Jorian. "That's what I said, is it not?" He looked down at the dead robber. "It behooves me to carry this rogue afar off, lest the corpse draw beasts of prey. He will soon stink in this heat anyway."

"Jorian!" said Karadur. "Ere you remove the body, should we not report this manslaying to someone in authority?"

"To whom?" said Jorian.

"Are we in Othomae or in Xylar?"

Jorian shrugged. "The boundary has never been surveyed so far south. When I was King of Xylar, I tried to persuade the Othomaeans to set up a joint boundary commission. But they suspected some swindle and made so many difficulties that I gave up. In sooth this lieu has no government and hence no law."

He relieved the body of its purse and weapons, hoisted it to his shoulders, and carried it back up the trail for a tenth of a league before dropping it and returning to the wagon.

During the rest of the day and all of the next, the cart was bedizened with bright paint and astrological symbols. Jorian shaved his face, and he and Margalit were turned a deep brown all over.

When it came Margalit's turn to be dyed, she said: "Jor-

141

ian, I pray you, go off and hunt something. I care not to have you staring whilst I stand nude before Father Karadur to be painted."

Jorian grinned. "If you insist; although he is a man, too."

"At his age, I do not feel the same as I should about you. You know wizards; he is probably centuries old."

"Folk exaggerate so!" said Karadur. "True, I may have somewhat lengthened my span by austerities and occult arts; but I have not yet reached a hundred."

"A wizard's life may or may not be centuries long," said Jorian. "But with so few amusements, it doubtless seems so in any case. Congratulations, Doctor. Here you are, at ninety-odd, looking like a limber lad of seventy!"

"Mock me not, saucy boy!" said Karadur. "Now take your crossbow and shoot us a hare or something, whilst I transform the lady."

The next morning they set out on the main road from Othomae to Xylar. Karadur took the name of Mabahandula, which he had used before. He wanted to give Jorian an equally polysyllabic Mulvanian name, but Jorian balked, saying: "It is all I can do to remember yours. Should we not feel silly if, when asked my own name, I had forgotten it?"

So Jorian became Sutru, while on Margalit was bestowed the name of Akshmi. Jorian wore a turban, a crimson jacket with many glass buttons, and baggy trousers gathered at the ankles, all bought from Henvin the Costumer. Margalit's Mulvanian garment was a broad, twenty-cubit length of thin material, wound round and round and over in a complicated way.

At a leisurely pace, they traveled through Xylar, stopping to pick up a few pence by fortune telling, juggling, and dancing. Margalit performed the dances that Jorian and Karadur had taught her, clattering finger cymbals while Karadur tapped a little drum and Jorian tweedled on a flute. His wound had become inflamed, making use of his left arm painful.

Jorian played such musical phrases as he could remember from Mulvan, repeating them over and over. Although Karadur muttered that generations of Mulvanian musicians would rise from their graves in fury at Jorian's treatment of their art, the villagers found nothing amiss. As Jorian pointed out, they had no standards of comparison. With practice the trio improved. The result, if not authentic Mulvanian art, was at least a good show.

On a day of heavy overcast, Karadur asked: "How far to the next village, my son?"

Jorian frowned. "That should be Ganaref, as I remember. By my reckoning, 'twill take us till after dark. I could get there sooner by spurring Cadwil, but Filoman shows signs of lameness. He needs a new off-front shoe; the smith in Othomae botched the job."

"Must we camp out again?" said Margalit.

"Belike not. The road to Castle Lorc branches off near here, and the castle would afford some shelter." He glanced up. "An I mistake not, we may have rain."

Karadur said: "Didst tell me, Jorian, that Baron Lorc's castle was haunted?"

"So it was reputed; I never looked into the matter. I pay little heed to such legends."

"Betimes you pay too little," said Karadur. Thunder rumbled.

Margalit and Karadur broke into speech at the same time. The Mulvanian urged that they turn off the road at once and rig their tent; the girl demanded that they press on to Ganaref. They were still arguing when Jorian said:

"Here, methinks, is the road to Castle Lorc."

Margalit peered from the cart. "It is half overgrown. Does none use it?"

"I suppose not. Here comes the rain!" A few large drops struck the canvas top of the cart. "That settles it; we spend the night in the castle. Hand me my cloak, somebody." Cloaked, he turned his horse on to the weedy track.

"I lust not to meet my ancestor's ghost," said Margalit.

"Are you a descendant of Baron Lorc?"

"Aye."

"Then, if ghost there be, it should be friendly. Come along!"

Trotting through the weeds and avoiding occasional small trees that had grown up in the road, they clopped through the forest up a long, easy slope. The rain began in earnest. Jorian was soon so wet that he decided it would serve no useful purpose to crawl into the cart.

At the top of the hill, the forest opened out into an area of low, thin second growth, where a wide greensward around the castle had been abandoned. Over the spindly little trees, black against the clouds, loomed the broken walls of the castle.

The front gate, fallen to pieces, admitted them to the courtyard. The yard was not only overgrown with weeds and a few saplings, which in their growth had pried up the cobblestones, but was also dotted with man-made pits, which the travelers had much ado to avoid.

"Treasure hunters have been here," said Jorian. "The folk of Ganaref have been here, too. They have taken the portcullis and a lot of the loose stones for their own uses. Let's see if enough roof is intact to keep off the rain. Wait whilst I search."

Jorian dismounted, handed the reins to Margalit, and strode into the castle, whose doors sagged on broken hinges. Inside, he had to climb over heaps of rubble where parts of the roof had fallen in. He moved warily.

At last he emerged, saying: "I've found a chamber that seems tight enough. Tie the animals to the statues around the fountain and come on in."

Jorian pulled the blankets and other gear out of the cart and carried the heaviest items in on his shoulders. He and his companions were no sooner settled than the rain stopped. The setting sun turned the undersides of the breaking clouds to crimson and purple.

"Damn it!" said Jorian, sneezing. "I wish I could get dry. Belike one of these fireplaces still draws. Luckily for us, the chimney had been invented in Lorc's time."

Jorian returned to the cart, got out the ax, and as twilight fell reappeared with an armful of slender logs. "This stuff is green and wet," he said. "You may have to use your fire spell again, Doctor."

* * *

They were still trying to light the fire when sounds from outside brought Jorian up. "Visitors," he muttered, rising and tiptoeing to the door. Returning, he whispered:

"Seven or eight, with horses; either robbers or treasure hunters. I could not be sure in this light, but two looked like those who ran from us near Moru. Margalit, would you get my sword? It is in the chamber with the rest of our gear."

"What good is one sword against eight rogues?" said Karadur. "You might earn a hero's death, but what would that avail us?"

"We must do something! They are standing about the wain and the beasts. Soon they'll come seeking us. Even if they fail to find us, they will take the cart and the animals."

"Here is your sword," said Margalit.

Karadur said: "Methinks we shall do better to afright them. Lady Margalit, pray fetch a blanket....Here!" He draped the blanket over Jorian's shoulders. "When they enter, do you impersonate the baron's ghost. Come back to the chamber, Margalit."

Soon, several armed men crowded into the crumbling hall. They glanced nervously about, looking up at the broken ceiling and the gallery that ran around the second story.

Draped in his blanket, Jorian stepped down the bottom steps of the stairway. As he emerged, he became barely visible in the deepening dark. In a sepulchrally deep voice, he said: "Who disturbeth the rest of Baron Lorc?"

As he spoke, he gripped the hilt of his sword beneath the blanket. If they saw through his disguise, they would not find him helpless. On the stair, they could not come at him more than two at a time.

The seven looked around with a hiss of sudden breaths. One uttered a low cry.

"Who violateth the demesne of Baron Lorc?" moaned Jorian, advancing a step.

The foremost man gave back. Another, turned and ran for the door, crying "Fly!" He stumbled over a loose stone, falling and scrambling up again.

145

In a trice, the other six also ran, tripping and stumbling. Jorian advanced by slow steps, in case one should look back in. From without came sounds of men hastily mounting, and a dwindling clatter of hooves. When Jorian got to the door, the courtyard was empty but for his horse, mule, and cart.

Jorian shrugged off the blanket and drew his forearm across his sweat-pearled forehead. "Come on out! They have fled!"

"I congratulate thee, young sir," said a voice behind Jorian. Jorian's hair prickled, for the voice was neither Karadur's high, nasal whine nor Margalit's clear contralto. Though faint and whispery, its tone was as deep as Jorian's own. He whirled, half drawing his sword.

A few paces away hovered a shadowy, translucent shape. It became the semitransparent figure of a short, stout, elderly man, clad in garments as antiquated as his speech.

Jorian started violently; his tongue seemed stuck to the roof of his mouth. At last he croaked: "Are—are you Baron Lorc? I m-mean, his ghost?"

"Aye, aye; in good sooth I am both. Thou hast most featly put to flight yon gang of scroyles and saved thy possessions. Had I not—"

The ghost broke off as Karadur and Margalit emerged from the stair passage. Jorian heard Margalit's catch of breath. Having somewhat regained his composure, Jorian remembered his current persona. Assuming his Mulvanian accent, he said:

"Exalted sir, these are traveling friends of me, dancer Akshmi and Doctor Maha—Mabahandula of Mulvan. I Sutru of Mulvan are. This Baron Lorc is."

Staring in the gloom, Margalit managed a wordless curtsey. The ghost smiled. "Thou seekest to cozen me to believe ye be Mulvanians. But I have harkened to you since ye entered my dilapidated manse, and I wot ye speak Novarian as do those born to the Twelve Nations. So I take it ye be merely Novarians in garb oriental. Now wherefore this imposture?"

Jorian sighed. "Well, I did but try. We are earning our way as entertainers from afar. Permit me to present the

146

Lady Margalit of Totens, who tells me she is a descendant of yours; and Doctor Karadur, who is truly a Mulvanian."

The ghost bowed, saying: "Indeed, it rejoiceth me to meet a kinswoman. I cannot kiss thy hand, for my form is insufficiently material; but I prithee, take the intention for the deed. I thank Zevatas that, after all these years, he hath allowed me visitors who flee not in terror from my aspect. Know that I am a harmless phantom, who findeth the lot of haunter a wearisome sameness. Will ye remain the night, keeping this lonesome wraith company and telling me somewhat of what hath befallen in the world of late? Since my friend Alaunus died, I have had no mortal copemate."

"Who was he?" asked Jorian.

"Alaunus was an aged drunkard, who lived by begging and promiscuous employment in Ganaref. Betimes he came hither to down a bottle and gossip with me. He was the only mortal for leagues hereabouts who feared me not."

"Why must you haunt this ruin, instead of going on to the afterworld?" asked Jorian.

"'Tis a long and heavy-footed tale. Were it not wiser to ignite your blaze and prepare your even's repast whilst I do speak? I were a poor host, to keep you standing. Take seats, an ye can find any that the tooth of time hath not destroyed."

When Jorian at last got the fire going and Margalit had spread out their modest supper, the baron resumed: "Now, where was I? Ah, yea; I was to relate the tale of my being bound to this place. Know ye that, in the last year of my mortal life, a wonderworker, clept Aurelion, appeared at the castle begging shelter. He was, he said, a wizard and alchemist. My health being bad, with disturbances of the heart, Aurelion said that, for a modest sum of gold, he would transmute lead into gold of ten times the quantity. Moreover, this alchemical gold was of such potency that, reduced to powder, it would cure all my ills and enable me to live on indefinitely.

"When my daughter and her husband came to visit, she warned me that the wight was but a charlatan. But so convincing was Aurelion's presence and so beguiling his

147

mien that I gave him the gold and commanded him to proceed forthwith.

"For the greater part of a twelvemonth, the alchemist dwelt in the castle, making, he said, his preparations. Ever he required more money to procure rare ingredients, some of which he went to Xylar City to obtain. He studied ancient books he had with him. He practiced magical operations in the tower of the castle that I had set aside for his use.

"As time passed, I became impatient with Aurelion's neverending flow of promises. At last I told him plain, either produce his gold or get himself hence, ere he eat me out of house and home. At last he announced that the final operation would take place the following night.

"That he was a true wizard or sorcerer as well as a cheat I have no doubt, the terms not being mutually exclusive. He evoked an authentic demon to assist him. Hath any of you witnessed a sorcerous evocation? Yea? Then I need not recount all the tedious details of the pentacle, the suffumigations, the chants, the gestures, and so forth. Suffice it to say that this fellow did place a hundredweight of bars of lead upon a table and performed a mighty conjuration thereover. When the smoke and flames cleared away, the bars did gleam with the aureate hue of authentic gold.

"Delighted was I with this addition to the familial fortune and even more so with the prospective banishment of the ills the flesh is heir to. Thinking but to test the softness of the gold, I stepped forward as soon as the metal had had time to cool, and thereupon did scratch one of the bars with my dagger. Ye may conceive my dismay when, at the touch of the steel, the bar instantly resumed the glaucous tones of lead. Fearing the worst, I speedily touched the other bars with my blade, and as I did so they in turn did lead once more become.

" 'Hah, sirrah, what is this?' I shouted at Aurelion, who in turn bawled at his demonic assistant: 'What's this, thou noodlehead? Thou hast cheated us!' The demon roared back: 'I did but follow thy commands, as I have done many

148

a time and oft before! 'Tis not my fault that this mortal detected thy cozening ere we had won clear!'

"Both wizard and demon screamed at each other until the demon vanished with a flash of light and a clap of thunder. I summoned the guards and bade them whip the alchemist from the castle.

"As he was being led, bound with ropes whilst two lusty guardsmen belabored his bare back till the blood flew, he snarled back at me: 'Baron Lorc, I curse thee with the curse of Gwitardus! When thou diest, thy spirit shall be bound to this castle until thou canst persuade a queen to scrub thy castle floor!'

"That was the last I saw of Aurelion. A few months later, my heart worsened, and one morn I arose to find I was looking down upon myself lying stark and still upon the bed. Then I wist that I had died in my sleep. I soon discovered that the alchemist's curse had come to pass, for my shade could not leave the castle.

"My daughter and her husband returned hither to carry out the funeral and the execution of my will. They moved into the castle for a time, since she was my principal heir. But, alas, whenever I sought converse with any person, that one became palsied with fright. My shade cannot be seen by full daylight; but as ye do observe, it becometh visible at night.

"Day or night, howsomever, none would linger to befriend a lonely old phantom. By day, they would hear a disembodied voice and run witlessly hither and yon, like unto a yard of fowls befrighted by the swoop of an eagle. At night they would run at the mere sight of me, whether or no I spake. Little by little the guards and other retainers departed to seek employment elsewhere. At last my daughter and son-in-law followed them forth, leaving me alone.

"At first I was not altogether discontented, for my wife had predeceased me, and I feared to encounter her in the afterworld. This prospect pleased me not a whit, by which hint ye may judge our state of marital felicity whilst she did live."

"You need not worry," said Karadur. "According to our savants, one is born into the afterworld virtually without memory of life in this one. Moreover, I am told that the people in that world number in the thousands of millions, wherefore the chances of your encountering your whilom spouse were too small to consider."

"Thou relievest my mind," said the ghost. "But, lacking a queen to scrub the floor, I know not how I shall ever attain that plane. I am like to spend all eternity here, whilst the castle crumbleth about me. Had I material hands, I would, an all else failed, make the repairs myself to stay the gaunt hand of decay. But as things be, what time doth not disintegrate, the treasure seekers rend asunder."

As the others ate, the ghost launched into a long account of his experiences in life: the year of a famine; his defense of the castle against a free company; and notable hunts in which he had taken part. He seemed a good-natured person of modest intelligence, limited experience, and somewhat narrow interests. He and Margalit got into a long discussion of genealogy, tracing her descent from him. There was talk of "Third Cousin Gerion," "Great-Aunt Bria," and other relatives whose names meant nothing to Jorian.

Then the garrulous ghost got off on the revolution in Xylar, several generations back, which had deprived the nobility of its feudal privileges. "A monstrous folly!" said the ghost. The baron spent the next hour fulminating against the injustice done his fellow lords and against the iniquities of the Regency Council, the true ruler of the nation ever since.

Jorian found the baron a nice enough fellow but a terrible bore. It took simultaneous yawns by the three travelers to remind the baron that, unlike him, mortals did from time to time require sleep.

✠✠✠✠✠✠✠✠✠✠✠✠✠✠✠✠✠✠✠✠

IX

THE
PROXENARY CLERK

"To address royalty in Mulvanian," said Karadur to Margalit, "one uses the politest form. Sentences whereof the ruler is subject or object are put in the third person singular subjunctive. For another member of the royal family, or a priest in his official capacity, one uses instead the third person singular indicative with the honorific suffix -ye—"

"Doctor," said Jorian, "we need not waste Margalit's time on these distinctions. Imprimus, we shan't perform before royalty; secundus, nobody in Xylar would know the difference anyway. Teach her the form used between equals and let it go at that."

"But, my son, if she is to impersonate a Mulvanian, she must not speak my beautiful mother tongue brokenly!"

"Jorian is right," said Margalit. "I find these lessons hard enough without more complications than are absolutely needed."

Karadur sighed. "Very well. Lady Margalit, suffer me to explain the significance of nasal vowels...."

"You had better compress your lessons," said Jorian. "Tomorrow we shall raise Xylar City. Meseems she already knows the sentences she will most need, such as 'I do not understand Novarian' and 'No thank you; my body is not for sale.'"

"Where are we stopping?" asked Margalit.

"Kerin and I have arranged to meet at the Fox and Rabbit."

The taverner, Sovar, looked suspiciously at the three exotic foreigners, but a deposit of a golden Xylarian lion quieted his fears. He gave them two rooms, a single for Margalit and a larger one for the two men. As they settled it, Jorian said to Karadur: "Doctor, pray ask our host if Synelius the Apothecary is still in business."

"Why me?"

"Because I am fain to keep out of sight. I patronized Synelius when I was king. If I ask after him and go to his shop, someone may put two and two together despite the costume and the bogus accent."

"What would you with this Synelius?"

"I wish some salve for this cut. My arm is still sore, and I want you to make the purchase."

"Ah, my old bones!" sighed Karadur, but he went. Later, when Jorian was applying the salve, Sovar knocked, saying: "A gentleman below asks after a party of Mulvanians. Be you they?"

"I will see," said Jorian. Below, he found his brother Kerin. Resisting an impulse to throw himself into a bear hug with his brother, Jorian clasped his hands in the Mulvanian manner and bowed low, murmuring: "Sutru of Mulvan, at your service. What can this unworthy one do for noble sir?" In a whisper he added: "Keep your voice down!"

Kerin, taking in his brother's costume and manner, compressed his lips in an effort not to burst into laughter. He said: "Ah, I understand. How about supper?"

"Nay; a Mulvanian cannot eat with a foreigner without pollution."

"I thought you told me," murmured Kerin, "you attended a party given by the Mulvanian emperor?"

"I did; but that was a dance, not a banquet. All they served was fruit juice, and I suppose that counts not." Raising his voice and resuming his accent, Jorian continued: "But do you chew by noble self, and then we will forgather in my humble quarters."

So Kerin ate by himself, while the pretended Mulvanians, eating their own supper, ostentatiously ignored him. Later, when only a few remained in the common room and those absorbed in their own affairs, Jorian caught Kerin's eye, winked, and gave a slight jerk of his head. After Jorian had disappeared into his room, Kerin rose and followed him up the stairs. In the room, they hugged and pounded each other's backs, grinning.

"Well?" said Jorian. "Can Thevatas deliver her?"

"So he claims. Have you it?"

"Aye; 'tis in yon bag atop my soiled garments. You can feel it through the cloth. When could he fetch her?"

Kerin shrugged. "Belike tomorrow even?"

"Make it earlier, at least an hour ere sunset. I am not lief to try to talk my way out of the city after the gates are closed for the night. When the palace finds she is gone, they'll swarm out like hornets."

As the sun approached the horizon, an increasingly nervous Jorian repeatedly stepped out of the Fox and Rabbit to look at the sky, or to walk down the street to glance at the water clock in the window of Vortiper and Jeweller.

At last, a worried-looking Kerin hastened up, murmuring: "Thevatas said he would be delayed."

"Why?"

"I'll tell you. Let us go inside. I'll wait in the common room, drinking beer; you shall return to your chamber. We would not make a public scene of this reunion."

"That's sense," said Jorian. "When did he say he'd be late?"

"I was to meet him in the Square of Psaan and guide

him hither, since I had not told him where you were staying. When he appeared not, I cast about the nearby streets, thinking there might have been a misunderstanding. I met him coming out of the apothecary's shop. When I asked about this, he said *she* had a headache and besought him to fetch her one of Synelius's simples. Hence they would be late."

Heart pounding, Jorian returned to his room, where he found Karadur and Margalit looking questions. "There's been a delay," he said shortly.

"But, my son," said Karadur, "darkness falls without, and the gates will close. How then shall we issue forth?"

"I wish I knew, too. Belike I can persuade or bribe the officer of the gate watch to open for us."

"Could we climb down the Doctor's magical rope from the city wall, as they do in romances?" asked Margalit.

"We could, but that would mean leaving the cart and the animals. Afoot, we should soon be run to earth."

"Were it not wiser to remain the night?" said Karadur. "In the morn, those who pass through the gates are not questioned."

"It would be, could we count upon Estrildis's disappearance to remain undiscovered. But someone is sure to sound the alarum. Then every guard, soldier, spy, and flunkey in Xylar will be out searching. They'll poke into every dog kennel and henhouse."

Karadur muttered, "We had better pray that this proxenary clerk and your Queen are stopped from leaving the palace. An they come hither, we are undone."

Jorian asked: "Could you send us to the afterworld, as you did me three years since?"

"Nay. That spell was one of the mightiest whereof I have command. It required extraordinary preparations, which took months. Ah well, they say beheading is one of the least painful forms of execution."

"Perhaps; but I have never heard a beheadee's side of the story."

"Anyway," said Karadur, "if they come seeking us, I will see what my illusion spells can accomplish."

"I can return to the palace, saying you snatched me thence, and I have only now escaped your captivity and made my way back to Xylar," Margalit suggested.

"That would not do," said Jorian. "Judge Grallon knows that you and I were on friendly terms in Othomae, not captor and captive. Mark you, if I must lose my head, it does not follow that you should lose yours. I can give the twain of you the names of other inns, not of the highest repute, where you will be taken in without questions. If men from the government question you, say you had no idea of who I really was."

"What about you?" said Margalit. "Why hide you not likewise?"

"I might; but let us first see whether Thevatas come hither, with or without Estrildis. Then we can better decide."

They went down to supper. Although Sovar's food was excellent, Jorian left half his repast uneaten. Kerin had returned to the Square of Psaan to await Thevatas. When one of Sovar's patrons became drunk and offensive, Jorian was tempted to beat the man up and pitch him out. Such was the tension within him that he felt he would burst if he could not discharge it in some violent action. With effort he controlled himself, and Sovar ejected the unruly patron.

Afterward they went back to the large room and sat gloomily, composing plan after plan to save their skins. They tried out various schemes, according to whether Thevatas came, with or without Estrildis, or did not come, or others came to arrest Jorian.

At last came a light tap on the door and Kerin's low voice: "Here they are!"

Jorian leaped up, overturning his chair, and threw open the door. Three stood in the door frame: the tall, handsome, youthful Kerin; a small, paunchy man of middle age; and a short woman in a hooded cloak, which fell to her ankles and hid her features.

"Come in!" whispered Jorian. He closed the door behind them and turned.

"Have you *it?*" said the small man.

"Aye. Is this *she?*" Jorian pulled back the hood. Estrildis's blond hair and round-featured face came into view. She seemed to stare unseeingly.

"Where is it?" demanded Thevatas. "I must begone, to establish my alibi."

Jorian dumped the contents of the bag out on the bed. He extracted the crown from the soiled clothing and handed it to Thevatas, who turned it over, hefted it, and put it back in its bag.

"Good!" muttered the clerk, turning to go.

"One moment!" said Jorian. "What mean you to do? Melt it down for bullion?"

"Nay; I have grander plans." The little man giggled. "Next time you visit Xylar, you shall find me a man of authority, perchance a member of the Regency Council. Meanwhile, keep your mouths shut, and I'll do likewise. Farewell!"

The clerk scuttled out and was gone. Jorian turned to Estrildis. "Darling!"

She turned her head slowly toward him but seemed unable to focus her eyes.

"What ails you, beloved?" Jorian asked.

She did not reply. Karadur said: "Your woman seems under some spell or drug. Smell her breath!"

Jorian sniffed. "There is something strange here.... How can we bring her round?"

Margalit grasped the girl by the shoulders and gave her a slight shake. "My lady! Your Majesty! Estrildis! Know you me not?"

"I have had some experience," said Karadur. "Suffer me to try."

He went to the washstand and dipped a corner of the towel in the water. Then he faced Estrildis and began slapping her cheeks gently with the wet towel, repeating her name.

Jorian untied the drawstring at Estrildis's throat and took off the enveloping cloak. His first impression was that his favorite wife had gained weight in the three years since they had parted. Then he looked more closely.

156

"Margalit!" he said. "Tell me honestly. Is she pregnant?"

Margalit stared at the floor. "Aye, she is."

"Did you know of this when the demon bore you off?"

"I had a strong suspicion. She had missed a period."

"When is the child due?"

"Methinks in a month or two."

"I cannot be the father. Who is?"

"I had liefer she told you," said Margalit.

Jorian turned back to Estrildis, who seemed to be coming round. Staring wide-eyed, she looked from one to the other, murmuring: "Where am I?" Then she shrieked: "Margalit! Do I dream?"

"Nay, dear one, it is I," replied Margalit.

"But what has made you so brown, like a nomad of Fedirun? Hast been lying all day in the sun?"

Jorian said: "Estrildis, dear!"

She stared at him in puzzlement. "Are you truly Jorian? And all brown, too?"

Jorian said: "You are at the Fox and Rabbit, in Xylar City. We came to fetch you away. But I see that things have changed."

For a long moment she stared wordlessly. Then she glanced down at her belly. "Oh, Jorian, I am so sorry! I could not help it."

"Who is he?"

"A young man of noble family, attached to the Regency."

"His name?"

"I—I won't tell. You would slay him, and I l-l-love him." She began to weep.

Jorian picked up the chair he had upset and sat down in it, burying his face in his hands. Then he said: "Sit down, the rest of you. We must think what to do."

Karadur said: "It is a shame we let that clerk make off with the crown ere we had looked into this matter."

"Spilt milk," said Jorian. "He'll be back at the palace by now, not to be dug out save by a siege. But he'd better not meet me on a dark night. Estrildis, did you wish to wed this other wight?"

"Aye; but the Regency would never dissolve my marriage to you whilst they had hope of luring you back to cut off your head."

Margalit asked: "Jorian, if you knew the father, would you kill him?"

Jorian heaved a deep sigh. "That was the first thought that entered my mind. But then...."

"And the second?"

"Then reason took hold. If I slew him, what should I have but a wife mourning her slain lover and rearing an infant not mine? I thought this would be the most loving reunion of history, but as things be.... Why did you not tell me ere this?"

Margalit spread her hands. "I could not foresee the outcome."

"How mean you?"

"Well, you might have died, or Estrildis might have died, or young Sir — the youth in question might have died. Then what good would it have done to tell you, save to make you unhappier than you need be? Besides, my first loyalty belonged to her. I did drop a hint or two."

"So you did. Did they companion often, those twain?"

"During the past year, he came to visit daily. After a while she asked me to leave them in privacy during these visits."

Jorian turned to Estrildis. "My dear, what has this young man that so turned your head?"

"Oh, he is handsome and brave and gallant, like a knight from feudal times. And he comes of noble family."

"You mean, like a knight as described in romances. We still have knights in Othomae. Some are not bad fellows; but others are mere bullies and lechers, who'll cut a commoner down over a fancied slight. And I am homely and hardworking and practical, and my forebears, like yours, were farmers and tradesmen. But tell me why, when Thevatas brought you hither, you acted drugged?"

"Because I had been. That rascal drugged me."

"How?"

"This afternoon he came, saying he could smuggle me out of the palace so I could rejoin my husband. But I refused. Much as I esteem you, Jorian, my heart belongs to—to the other."

"What then?"

"Thevatas went away. After supper he came back, saying he had obtained a pot of rare tea from the Kuromon Empire. He carried the pot wrapped in a towel to keep it warm and invited me to join him. I thought it tasted strange, and the next thing I knew, I was in such a daze that I knew not what I did. I remember Thevatas's wrapping me in that peasantly cloak and guiding me out, telling the guards I was a light leman of his."

Kerin said: "That explains what Thevatas was doing at the apothecary's."

Jorian sat silently as the others watched. Their expressions mingled curiosity, expectancy, and a trace of fear. At last he said:

"I see no way out of this tangle but to cut our losses and run. Kerin can take Estrildis back to the palace gate and leave her there. She can make up her own taradiddle of having walked out by a ruse, to wander the city unescor—"

A sharp knock interrupted. Jorian picked up his scabbarded sword from where it leaned in a corner, drew the blade, and faced the door, muttering:

"If that's the Regency's bully-rooks, they shan't take me alive. Stand back, all! Come in, whoever you are! It is not bolted."

A slim, strikingly handsome man, several years younger than Jorian, stood in the doorway. At the sight of Jorian's blade, he said: "Ha!" and reached for his own hilt.

"Corineus!" cried Estrildis.

Jorian backed a step. "Another mystery explained. Well, come on in and close the door! Stand not there like a ninny!"

The young man drew with a *wheep*. He entered, saying: "I perceive you wish to slay me to wipe the stain from your honor. So, have at you!" He took the guard position.

"You mistake me," said Jorian. "I know about you and my wife, but I do not wish to cause unnecessary sorrow or to leave the child fatherless. Neither do I wish the task of rearing it. So take her and it; they are yours."

Sir Corineus frowned in puzzlement. "Did I hear you aright? Methought Jorian was brave, not an arrant coward."

"My bravery has nought to do with it. If we fight, either I shall slay you, or you will kill me. I am not eager to be slain just yet; and as for slaying you, what would that profit me? What could I get for your carcass? Your hide were of little value as leather, and we don't eat our fallen foes as in Paalua."

"You have no knightly sense of honor! You sound like a mere tradesman, a cold, scheming, money-grubber!"

Jorian shrugged. "Suit yourself. If you attack me, I'll give a good account of myself; but I shan't be sorry if you refrain."

"It is plain that you are no gentleman, or you would have demanded instant satisfaction when I implied you were a coward."

"My dear boy, you are living in the past! Those ideas have been obsolete in Xylar for a century."

"To you, belike, but not to me. How much must I insult you ere you fight me?"

"You try my patience, young man, but I'll essay to be reasonable. Wherefore are you so avid to fight?"

"Because, so long as you live, I cannot wed Estrildis. So one of us must die. Have at you again!" And Corineus rushed forward, aiming a slash at Jorian.

In an instant they were furiously hacking and thrusting. Sparks flew from the flickering blades. The others crowded against the far wall to keep out of harm's way.

Jorian found that Corineus was a fair but not a first-class fencer. He beat off the young man's frenzied attacks until Corineus, panting and sweating, began to flag. Then Jorian made a quick feint and a slash at the top of Corineus's head. The blade bit into the youth's scalp, but the blow was not hard enough to disable him. Corineus backed off to wipe from his forehead the trickle of blood that ran down from the scalp wound.

Jorian was not yet breathing hard. Presently Corineus

came on again, more slowly and carefully. He got his point into the sleeve of Jorian's shirt, opening a rip.

"Another sewing job, Margalit," said Jorian. Again he feinted, doubled, and brought his blade down on Corineus's pate. Corineus backed off, wiping a fresh flow of blood from his scalp. His face was becoming smeared with blood.

They fenced on indecisively until both simultaneously attempted an advance-thrust and found themselves in a *corps-à corps*, with blades crossing near the hilts. For an instant they struggled frozen in position, each trying to push the other off balance.

By sheer strength, Jorian forced the other blade up and back, until he could bring his own blade down on Corineus's mangled scalp again. He sawed two more gashes in the flesh. Corineus staggered back and disengaged, frantically wiping his face with his free hand.

It was no use. Blinded by the flow of blood, Corineus stood helplessly, pawing at his face. Jorian whacked his sword hand with the flat of his blade. Corineus's sword clattered to the floor. Jorian put a toe beneath it, tossed it into the air, and caught it.

A knock sounded, and Sovar's voice said: "Is all well within, gentlemen?"

"All's well," replied Jorian. "We did but practice." He turned to the others. "See if you can bandage this poor fellow. Sit down, Corineus."

"Where? I cannot see."

Jorian pushed Corineus into a chair. The youth said: "You have made a mock of me! My honor is in ruins! I must seek an honorable death to atone for my disgrace."

"Oh, for the gods' sake!" snorted Jorian. "Play the man for once and not the silly child!"

"What would you of me?"

"Tell me more of this affair. How did you find us here?"

"I saw Thevatas leaving the palace with Estrildis, whom I knew despite that cloak. The eye of true love sees through all disguises. I followed until the clerk entered the inn. I waited without, trying to decide whether to alert the Regency Council or to cope with the matter myself. After

Thevatas emerged and hastened furtively away, I decided it were a more honorable and knightly course to essay the rescue myself. So here I am."

"Lucky for us, young man," said Jorian. "I cannot fight the whole garrison single-handed. Now then, you claim the title of 'Sir.' Why is that?"

Corineus nursed the hand that Jorian had struck, on which an angry bruise was rising. "As you surely know, it is a title accorded sons of a hereditary baron, since we have no true orders of knighthood any longer. My sire, Lord Holdar, is titular baron of Maesbol."

"I know of that family. What do you for a living?"

"I am undersecretary in the foreign department."

"Maesbol is close to the borders of Ir, is it not?"

"Aye."

"Does your father dwell thereabouts?"

"Aye, we still have a small castle and enough land to support it, albeit we are much fallen from our former estate. No longer can we compel hinds to swink in our fields as their feudal duty, but must hire these oafs for real money, like any untitled squire."

"Tsk, tsk," said Jorian. "Having worked as a hind, I sympathize with the oafs. But do you love Estrildis enough to give up your post in the govenment?"

"Aye! What true knight would not—"

Jorian held up a hand. "Has your father influence with the syndics of Ir?"

Corineus looked puzzled. "Aye, now that you mention it. Those money-grubbers buy our surplus crops. Why?"

"Why not take Estrildis to Ir and, with some hidden influence from your father, get your marital status sorted out? When things quiet down and you and she are legally joined—at least under Irian law—you can slip back to your father's estate and work for him. If he makes difficulties, the sight of an infant grandchild should soften him."

"But what of you, King Jorian?"

Jorian grinned. "No titles, pray. As you said, I am a tradesman at heart. I shall manage, albeit differently from your way."

Corineus shook his head, muttering: "I do not understand this modern world. In feudal times, every man knew his place and what he must do to defend his honor. In our bout just now, you could have slain me six times over; I knew it almost as soon as we engaged. Yet you refrained, as though I were nought but a bad-tempered child."

"To slay you once would have been sufficient; and had I been full of your ancient notions of honor, I had done just that. But let us be practical. Have you means of reaching Ir? Estrildis is in no condition to ride horseback."

Corineus pondered. "My friend Vercassus has a gig, which he has lent me in times past. Belike I can borrow it. I keep my horse in Vercassus's stable, and my groom Gwithion sleeps in the servants' quarters there. I can take both with me to Maesbol, and my man can return the gig to Vercassus. If Gwithion have not gone out on a round of the mughouses, we should be ready to fly within the hour."

"How will you get out of the city at night?"

"The captain of the watch at the North Gate owes me a gambling debt. Now, if you will excuse me whilst I return to the palace for my belongings—"

"Better not take time for that. Belongings can be replaced, but your head cannot. And pray take Estrildis to your friend's house forthwith, for our safety here."

Corineus seemed inclined to argue, but Jorian said firmly: "Nay, out you go, the twain of you. As the little clerk said, keep your mouths shut and we'll keep ours likewise. Good-bye, Estrildis."

She began to weep again. "I know not what to say—it is awkward—you are a true gentleman despite what he said—"

"Na, na, forget all that and get tha hence," said Jorian, reverting to the rustic Kortolian dialect of his boyhood. "Partings, like executions, were best done speedily; but a shall remember ma bonny little farm lassie."

Wrapped in the hooded cloak, Estrildis went out sniffling. Corineus shepherded her, treating her as if she were a fragile glass vase.

* * *

163

"Whew!" Jorian drew his sleeve across his forehead. "Let us hope they get safely away ere the palace come looking for them. Think you not that we need a draft of Sovar's best? All but Father Karadur, whose principles forbid."

"I'll fetch the wine," said Kerin.

"Methinks even I could bend my principles a trifle," said Karadur. "This is a change from how you formerly spoke, Jorian, of skewering any villain who so much has made eyes at your lass."

"That's your doing," said Jorian. "I remembered your lecture, when we were flying over the Lograms. So I've tried in accordance therewith to take the long view of what were best for all concerned. Corineus would call that unknightly, but happily I have no knightly code to live up to. The lad may be handsome and brave and gallant, but he is also a damned fool."

Margalit said: "That's the main reason I insisted on coming on this journey."

"How mean you?" said Jorian.

"Methought that, when you learned of her infidelity, you might slay her in your rage; and I thought it my duty to protect her. Thank Zevatas I did not have to throw myself betwixt her and your steel!"

For the next hour they sat in the large bedchamber, drinking from the bottle that Kerin had brought and talking plans. Then, bottle empty, Kerin spoke of returning to his quarters and Margalit, of retiring to her chamber. They were bidding good night when a noise from below caught their attention. There were footfalls of many men, a rumble of speech, and a clank of weapons.

Kerin looked out, then softly closed the door. "It's a squad of the Royals, looking for *her*," he said. "They will search every digit of this place, their officer says. What now?"

"Let me think," said Jorian. "If we try to run for it—nay; and if they look us over closely, they may see that Margalit and I are disguised....I know one trick that might throw them off. Kerin and Karadur, get under the bed! Margalit, take off your clothes and get into the bed!"

"What!" she cried. "Art mad? Why—"

"Just do it! I'll explain anon." As he spoke, Jorian peeled off his own garments. "Hasten, curse it! Fear not for your virtue; this is but a charade to cozen them. Yare!"

"Every last stitch?" quavered Margalit, unwinding the voluminous Mulvanian garment.

"Every stitch!" Standing naked, Jorian waited until Margalit was under the blanket, while his brother and Mulvanian were out of sight beneath the bed. Then he blew out the lamp and slid under the blanket. Below, Kerin grunted as Jorian's weight pressed the bed down upon him. "Quiet!" whispered Jorian, sliding an arm around Margalit, who stiffened at his touch. "Let me do the talking."

The tramping and voices outside went on and on. At last the door burst open. Turning his head, Jorian made out the silhouette of two Royal Guardsmen in the doorway. Half sitting up, still holding Margalit closely, he roared:

"Heryx smite you with emerods! Cannot a man make love to his own lawful wife in privacy? Have you no decency? Get out!"

"I beg your pardon, sir," said a voice. The door closed, and the trampings died away. When all sounds of the visitations ended, Jorian got out of bed, opened the door a crack to peek out, and relit the lamp.

"They've gone," he said, pulling on his trousers.

Margalit held the Mulvanian garment against her front. "May I go now?"

"Aye, my dear. If any wight besmirch your fair name as a result of this play-acting, Kerin and the Doctor can swear I took no liberties. They'd have known."

"But you thought of those liberties. I could tell." She giggled. "After traveling about with you, Jorian, I misdoubt I have any fair name left to preserve."

X

THE HAUNTED CASTLE

Margalit, handling Filoman's reins, said: "Jorian, for one whose heart has just been broken by his love's faithlessness, you seem unwontedly cheerful."

Jorian, riding Cadwil beside the cart, had been singing an air from *The Good Ship Petticoat*, by Galliben and Silfero:

> "Oh, I am a pirate captain bold;
> I fill my vessel with jewels and gold
> And slaughter my captives, young and old,
>   To rule the raging sea, oh!"

He gave Margalit a searching look, saying: "You are right, now that I bethink me. It was a shock, of course. But later, when I pondered the matter, along with my grief, disappointment, and resentment, I realized there was an element of relief."

"Meaning you loved her not so desperately as you have been alleging?"

"Well, three years is a long separation for one so young

166

and lusty as Estrildis. True. I loved her—I still do in a way—and had she remained true, I would have tried to be a loving, faithful husband. When she did not, I found the break less painful than I might have expected. Mean you to return to your post at the Academy?"

"Aye; what else? There are few positions as a queen's lady-in-waiting open."

They had been traveling southeasterly, wasting no time but not moving so hurriedly as to arouse suspicion. Once a squadron of horse caught up with them and searched them. But Jorian's Mulvanian accent, together with the lack of any trace of Estrildis, convinced the troopers that these were merely harmless foreigners. They galloped on.

Jorian said: "We shall soon come to the road to Castle Lorc. Let's spend the night there. Baron Lorc is not a bad sort as ghosts go, and we shall have a roof over our heads."

When neither of his companions objected, Jorian led the cart up the long, overgrown slope to the ruined castle. Margalit called: "Jorian! Had we not better station the cart and the beasts behind the castle, instead of in the courtyard? They were less visible."

"That's my wise woman! How have I managed without you all these years?"

"Welcome, my friends," said Baron Lorc's ghost, as darkness fell and Margalit set out their supper in the main hall. "Let me think. The large man, albeit clad as a Mulvanian, saith he be Nikko of Kortoli. The lady is Margalit of Totens; and—I forget thy name, reverend sir. If thou hast noted a failure of memory with advancing age, thou mayst imagine how much worse it be for me."

"He is Doctor Karadur," said Jorian.

"Now, this doth excite mine interest," said the ghost. "Ye see, yesternight a squadron of cavalry made free with my demesne, and I overheard their talk. Several troopers seemed not to know what their mission portended, having been mere boys when these events began. So their officer related the particulars.

"It transpired that they sought one Estrildis, Queen of Xylar, who hath vanished. The burthen was that she had been abducted by her husband, the fugitive King Jorian, who disappeared three years since. He fled, they said, to escape beheading at the ceremony that taketh place every lustrum—or would, had not Jorian's desertion thrown the calendar into confusion."

"We heard something of that," said Jorian.

"Ah, but that was not all. According to this officer, this Jorian also passeth under the name of Nikko of Kortoli, to which name thou didst admit when I confronted thee with proof thou wert no true Mulvanian. Now, were that not a coincidence singular? And furthermore, this officer spake of one Margalit of Totens, once lady-in-waiting to Queen Estrildis, who vanished last winter—some say carried off by a demon, but the officer believed not that tale—and hath not been seen since. One such coincidence of names were within the realm of the possible; but *two!* That passeth all bounds of rational belief."

Jorian sighed. "Very well, I confess—again. Means this that you will set the next group of searchers on our trail?"

"Nay; why should I? But what in sooth hath befallen the Queen? I see her not with thee."

"She has gone off in another direction, with one who, she hopes, will become her new husband."

The ghost shook its transparent head. "I regret that she came not with thee. Then ye could set me free from this curse."

"You mean, if Estrildis would scrub the floor?"

"Yea, verily. Be ye still wedded, thou and she?"

"Legally, I believe so. She hopes to arrange a divorce in another state, since Xylar won't give her one."

The ghost frowned, chin in hand. "A new thought doth begin to blossom in my brainpan, or whatever phantoms have in lieu thereof. In life I was the local magistrate, and none hath ever canceled my appointment. I can grant thee a divorce. Her refusal to accompany thee maketh her guilty of desertion."

"Is a legal act by a ghost valid?"

"I misdoubt the point hath ever come before thy high courts. But let us assume it so be. Then thou couldst wed the Lady Margalit here. Since thou art King, thy consort is Queen. So if she scrub my floor—not all of it, I do assure thee—I were instanter enlarged from this durance tedious."

Jorian and Margalit stared at each other. "Well!" said Jorian at last. "That's an interesting suggestion. We should need time to consider it."

Margalit said nothing. The baron said: "All the time ye wish, gentles. I would not coerce you into hasty acture. But think: once I am suffered to depart for my next life, ye need no more worry about my betraying you to the Xylarians! A favor meriteth a return favor."

"Let's sleep on it," said Jorian.

Next morning, Jorian said: "Margalit, let's take a walk and see how our beasts fare."

When they had found the horse and the mule thriving, Jorian looked at Margalit. "Well?"

"Well, what?" she replied.

"You know. The baron's proposal that you and I wed."

"Mean you that you do not altogether trust this ghost? That, if we yield not to his urgings, his resolution not to betray us might weaken? He hinted as much."

"That was a consideration; but it is not what I had in mind."

"What had you in mind?"

Jorian kicked a stone from the path. "I had not meant to speak thus but three days after parting from Estrildis. I have been drawn to you ever since the demon fetched you to Abacarus's sanctuary. You have all I should wish for in a life's companion, including the good sense that I, alas, sometimes lack. When I see you dance in your Mulvanian guise, 'tis all I can do not to leap up and bear you off.

"Ere the break with Estrildis, I told myself: Jorian, you are a faithful husband who'll do aught to recover his beloved wife. What you feel for Margalit is mere lust. But now I cannot deny that I am in love with you. I had meant, after a decent interval, to press my suit; but the baron has forced my hand.

"True, this journey has made a beggar of me, since

Thevatas got away with the crown. But I have always been able to earn a living in one way or another."

"How legal would such a marriage be?" she asked. "I have heard of taking a ghost's deposition in a lawsuit, but never of one's acting as magistrate. Even if the marriage were legal, a royal divorce might not be, since the Regency claims authority in such matters."

"Well," said Jorian, "if I be King, then by Xylarian law I am entitled to five wives. So I cannot be faulted for bigamy whatever Estrildis's status. At least, that is, in Xylar, whither I hope never to return. How think you?"

"Jorian, promise me one thing."

"Aye?"

"That as soon as we cross into Othomae—assuming they do not catch us—you will file similar actions for divorce and marriage under Othomaean law, so that no awkward questions shall arise."

"Mean you that your answer be 'yea'?"

"Aye, I do so mean. Well?"

"I promise. And back in Kortoli I'll do it again!"

Told of the betrothal, Karadur said: "My felicitations on you twain. But it does seem a pity that all your arduous efforts, over the last three years, to regain your spouse should come to nought."

"Rubbish, old man!" snapped Jorian. "My efforts have given me an infinitude of stories to tell. And without these attempts, I should never have known Margalit. So from adversity has come treasure."

"As to that, we shall judge ten years hence."

"No doubt; but I can't wait until we are all dead ere making up my mind. Let's to it."

Under Baron Lorc's directions, Jorian found some yellowing papers in the desk in the baron's cabinet. With the ghost invisibly dictating, Jorian wrote legal phrases on them. He signed the first, and both he and Margalit signed the second. The problem was getting the baron to sign, since the ghost was not material enough to grasp Jorian's quill pen. At last, by concentrating his psychic force, the ghost made a small scorch mark on each of the sheets where his signature would have appeared. Jorian, Margalit, and Karadur signed their names around the blackened spots as witnesses to Baron Lorc's mark.

"Hail!" said the disembodied voice. "Now stand ye before me—"

"Where is that?" asked Jorian.

"Oh, pox! Anywhere will do. Stand side by side and clasp hands. Dost thou, Jorian...."

The ceremony was soon over. The ghost said: "Now, sir and madam, I pray you to carry out your side of the bargain. Goodwife Margalit, thou shalt find a bucket in the kitchen, and the well still holdeth water. For a rag, thou must needs employ something from thine own possessions, for the looters have swept the castle clean of aught of that sort."

They made a rag by cutting a piece off the tail of Jorian's older shirt. Margalit got down on her knees and scrubbed. After a few moments, the invisible ghost said:

"That will suffice, my dear. The curse is lifted; I do perceive the walls of the castle fading from view.

"Oh, ere I depart, one small matter. The treasure hunters have poked and pried all over my poor castle. If ye covet the small hoard they sought but never found, pry out a stone to the right of the main fireplace: third course from the bottom, second stone from the left. 'Tis of no use to me. And now fare ye well! I am...." The voice faded to silence.

Jorian pried the stone loose, disclosing a hollow containing a bag of coin. When counted, the hoard came to ninety-nine Xylarian lions plus some small change.

"Ha!" said Jorian. "'Tis almost exactly the sum wherewith I fled from Xylar the first time. 'Twill not buy an army or a kingdom, but at least we shan't starve for a while!"

Four days later, riding through broad farmland, Jorian said: "We should reach the Othomaean border by nightfall. We could get there sooner by hard driving, but I like not the look of Filoman's leg."

They were seated beside the road, eating. Karadur said:

171

"Silence, I pray." His dark eyes took on a glassy, faraway look.

Jorian whispered: "He is listening for some message from the astral plane."

At last the old Mulvanian shook his head. "My son," he said, "my second sight informs me that we are again pursued."

"How far? How many?"

Karadur shook his head. "I cannot say at the distance, save that they approach swiftly."

Jorian wolfed down his last mouthful. "Finish up, my dears, and let us to horse—or to mule."

Soon they were again trotting along the road to Othomae. An hour later, Karadur said: "I caught another glimpse. I estimate them as not above two leagues behind us."

"Jorian," said Margalit, "why do you not gallop on, leaving us? We can turn into some side road and let them go past. We must not slow your steed to a trot, when you can reach the border safely ahead of them."

"And leave you to their mercies? Be not silly, wife!" snorted Jorian. "Besides, this country is too open for playing hide-and-seek with pursuers. They'd see you in no time."

"Then," said Karadur, "why not mount Margalit on the horse behind you and gallop on? I can drive the cart, and if they stop me, I am but a poor fortune-teller who knows naught of Xylar and its fugitive kings. I can change my appearance by a small illusion spell. What ails that plan?"

"Two things," said Jorian, speeding up his trot while Margalit lashed Filoman to hasten the placid mule. "Imprimus, Margalit's weight would slow Cadwil almost as much as my staying with the cart. She's a big girl. Secundus, we have been seen together enough so that they'll be looking for you as well as me."

"Belike," said Margalit, "they would not punish us severely. Karadur and I could say you deceived us."

"Count not upon the Regency's mercies. At the least, you would likely spend most of your lives in dungeons dank. If anyone shall play fox to their hounds, 'tis I. Karadur is small and slight. You and he together weigh no more than I. You twain could gallop in tandem to the border, trusting me to dodge or cozen the puruers."

"Nay!" said Karadur. "My old bones are too brittle for such a dash. The mere thought of perching precariously atop your great destrier makes me dizzy."

"Well, we had better do something, and speedily," said Jorian. "Try your astral vision again."

Karadur closed his eyes. After a while he said: "They are less than a league behind us. I make ten or twelve."

Margalit: "Perchance they are not concerned with us."

Jorian shook his head. "They would not push their beasts so hard, save in flight or pursuit."

For several minutes they trotted as briskly as the pace of the cart allowed. As they topped a rise, Jorian called out: "Ha! I see woods! I remember now; when I was King, this tract was the subject of a lawsuit betwixt a syndicate of magnates, who wished to cut the timber, and the Xylarian Navy, who wished to preserve the forest for future ship timbers."

"How did you decide?" asked Margalit.

"Grallon decided for the Navy, and I supported him. It was a close thing. He might have ruled the other way had not one of the magnates made the error of trying to bribe him, as Abacarus did lately."

"What then? Mean you to hide in the forest?"

"Nay; the tract is not large enough. But—Karadur, you have your magical rope, do you not?"

"Aye. But its magical charge is nearly exhausted. After two or three more usages, it will require to be ensorcelled again."

"Canst use it against our pursuers?"

"I can inflict a painful overthrow upon them, but that will not necessarily slay them."

"I would not fain kill the poor fools, but I urgently yearn to get my hands on their commander. Here is what we shall do...."

Half an hour later, the cart had been pulled well off the road and concealed behind several saplings. Jorian had cut

173

these with his sword, trimmed them at the butt end to points, and thrust them into the ground. Out of sight behind the cart, the horse and the mule were tethered.

Karadur unwound the rope from his waist and tossed it so that it lay athwart the road. He muttered an incantation, and the two ends of the rope groped around until they found tree trunks. These ends, like questing serpents, then crept up the trunks and wound around them. The bulk of the rope still lay limply, hardly visible, in the dust.

They waited for what seemed hours to Jorian but was in fact less than half an hour. Then the squadron of horse appeared on the road, coming at a tired gallop. The panting horses were flecked with foam from hard riding. Jorian suspected that some would never be good cavalry mounts again; they had been used up.

On came the soldiers, in scarlet coats under their mail shirts, the afternoon sun flashing from their silvered helmets. The lieutenant, distinguishable by the little silver wings on his helm, rode in the lead.

"Now!" breathed Jorian.

Behind him, Karadur muttered another spell. At once the ends of the rope coiled around the tree trunks came to life, like serpents constricting their prey. The bulk of the rope rose from the dust to stand as a rigid horizontal bar at knee height.

The rope snapped into position just as the lieutenant's horse reached it, so the rider had no chance to jump his mount over this not very formidable barrier. The horse did a somersault, throwing the lieutenant ahead of him into the dirt. With a hideous clatter, the following horses piled up in a kicking heap.

Before any of the thrown soldiers had time to rise, Jorian leaped out from behind his tree and sprinted to where the lieutenant had fallen. As he arrived, the man was sitting up with a dazed look. One of the silver wings on his helmet was crumpled.

Jorian seized the lieutenant around the neck from behind and pressed his dagger against the young man's throat. "Order them back!" he roared, "or you're a dead man!"

Those soldiers who had regained their feet paused, taking in the situation. So did the three troopers who had pulled up their mounts in time to keep their saddles. Of the fallen soldiers, one lay still with his neck twisted; another was calling out something about a broken arm. Others nursed lesser injuries.

"Stand back!" wheezed the lieutenant. "Do nought to disturb this man!" He turned his head a little. "Are you King Jorian?"

"Never mind who I am. You shall come with me as hostage. Karadur!"

"Aye, my son?"

"Give your rope that other command."

Karadur muttered another spell. The rope came alive, snaking out from under a fallen horse and slithering to where Jorian held the lieutenant. The rope coiled around the captive's wrists and ankles. In a trice the lieutenant was tied as securely as a hog on the way to market.

"Order them to return to their quarters!" said Jorian. "And tell them that, the instant I see we are again pursued, away goes your tender young throat!"

The lieutenant repeated the command. The soldiers gathered in a group, arguing in low, tense tones. Jorian guessed that they were debating whether to ignore the officer's orders, as given under duress, and try to seize Jorian anyway. Jorian suspected that he had some sympathizers, who would be glad to see him escape.

At last the soldiers mounted and rode off, the dead man draped across his saddle and another with his arm in a sling.

"I regret that young man's death," said Jorian. "One would think you people would learn that seeking to lay violent hands on me entails risks."

"I do my duty," rasped the lieutenant between set teeth.

Margalit led Jorian's horse from the woods, and Karadur followed with the mule and cart. Jorian boosted Lieutenant Annyx, whose horse had gone off with the rest of the troop, into the cart. Margalit said:

"Jorian, do you go through life taking hostages? In the short time I've known you, you have done it thrice already."

Jorian shrugged. "Only when I must. Forsooth, I never took them ere meeting you; that is just how events have fallen out."

The sun was a crimson ball on the horizon when Jorian came in sight of the fence marking the border between Xylar and Othomae. A Xylarian border guard was closing the gate on the Xylarian side but opened it again as Jorian and his party appeared. The guards gave them a bored, perfunctory glance, not inspecting the cart, wherein Lieutenant Annyx lay bound, gagged, and covered by a blanket. The horse and mule proceeded into the neutral strip, three or four fathoms wide, between the two nations. At the far end of this strip stood another fence and gate.

In the neutral strip, Jorian halted, reached into the cart, and hauled out Lieutenant Annyx. "Turn him loose," he told Karadur.

The Mulvanian incanted; the rope fell limply to the ground. Karadur gathered it up and wound it around his waist.

Annyx arose with murder in his eyes and tore the gag loose. As Jorian led his horse to the second gate, the lieutenant shouted:

"Seize that man! He is wanted in Xylar! He is a violent criminal, a kidnapper, a fugitive from justice!"

The officer of the border watch on the Othomaean side said: "Send us a formal request for extradition, laddie, and we'll see what we can do."

The lieutenant looked as if he could cry. "You damned Othomaeans never do aught we ask, no matter how reasonable! This is a flagrant case of hot pursuit, so I am entitled to demand your aid in apprehending him!"

The Othomaean grinned. "That's the first time I ever heard a man who has been carried hog-tied in a cart claim he was in hot pursuit of anyone." He turned to Jorian. "And you, my fine oriental friend, what is your business in the Grand Duchy?"

Pulling Annyx's sword and dagger out of the cart, Jorian tossed them back into the neutral zone. He got out his papers. "Here you are, sir: permit for a foreigner to reside

176

in Othomae; permit to wear a sword; permit to hunt and fish. As for the costume, I had business in Xylar and wished to do it without losing my head."

"Jorian of Ardamai!" exclaimed the guard. "We hear fantastic tales of you. Is it true that you slew a unicorn in the Grand Duke's park with your bare hands?"

"Not quite," said Jorian. "If I remember—"

Lieutenant Annyx had picked up his weapons. He shouted: "I demand—"

"Oh, shut thy gob!" said the Othomaean officer. "This man is well known in Othomae and, from all I hear, is entitled to political asylum. Now go away like a good boy and cease to pester us."

"You shall hear more of this!" said Annyx, turning back to the Xylarian side.

"The first inn," said Jorian, "is a league or so down the road. May we be on our way, to reach it ere dark?"

Two years later, a small party appeared at the entrance to Evor's Sons, Clock-Makers, in Kortoli City. A foppishly dressed young man asked if Jorian were in. Sillius, the senior man of the firm, said:

"My brother is in but busy. May I have your name and business?"

"I am Corineus son of Holdar, and I bring a message from the Provisional Government of Xylar."

Sillius's eyebrows rose. "Wait, good my sir," he said, and disappeared. Soon he returned, saying: "I will show you the way in."

Corineus found himself in a large room used as a workshop. Tables were littered with tools and with sheets of paper bearing diagrams and sketches. In a chair at one end sat a tall, handsome woman nursing a year-old baby. At the other, Jorian, wearing a workman's leather apron over his clothes, puttered with a device of gears and levers.

It took Corineus a few heartbeats to recognize Jorian. When they met in Xylar, Jorian was clean-shaven and turbaned, with a dark-brown skin. Now he was light-skinned, bare-headed, and bearded. Corineus noted that he had put on weight, and that his black hair had receded a little.

"Your Majesty!" cried Corineus at last.

Jorian looked up. "By Imbal's iron yard!" he cried. "What brings you hither, Corineus? If you think to kidnap me back to Xylar to cut off my head again, forget it. I have taken measures."

"Nay, nought like that," said Corineus. "We have had a revolution and abolished the Regency Council, along with the custom of lustral regicide. We have a new constitution, with a king of limited powers and an elective legislature. And we want you for King!"

"Well, dip me in manure!" After a pause, Jorian smiled. "Tell them I thank them, but nay. I have all I wish right here." He glanced toward Margalit, who smiled back. "Tell them to find some other popinjay, intelligent enough to follow public rituals but not so clever as to plot to seize absolute power."

"But King Jorian! My liege lord!" pleaded Corineus, sinking to one knee. "You are famous! You have become our national hero! The tale of your adventures—slaying the dragon single-handed, overthrowing the Goblin Tower, routing the besiegers of Iraz—is worth an epic by Physo!"

"I see the tales have not shrunk in the telling. Get some poet to make a lay, then, and send me a copy. 'Twere good for business."

"Business!" said Corineus in tones of disgust. "After all your splendid adventures, do you not find a mere tradesman's life dull?"

Jorian laughed. "Not at all, my dear fellow. As you once said, I am a tradesman at heart. We prosper. I have the respect of my workfellows, the love of my dear ones, plenty to eat and drink, and money at usury with my banker. My wife, by doing the bookkeeping, keeps us solvent.

"Furthermore I am engaged in a problem more fascinating to me than how far one must run to tire out a pursuing dragon."

"What's that?"

"To make an accurate clock powered by falling weights instead of falling water. I saw them working on such in Iraz. My little brother Kerin has gone to the Far East to learn the secret of their superior escapement."

178

Corineus shook his head. "I cannot imagine how one who has survived all your knightly adventures could settle down to so drab a life."

Jorian: "Since I survived those adventures by the skin of my teeth, they make fine fireside talk. But I sought them not; the goddess Elidora forced them upon me. Whilst they were going on, I should have been heartily glad to be elsewhere. Meseems that when one has had as many narrow escapes as have been crowded into the first half of my life, one is happy to spend the second half in a safe, peaceful, humdrum pursuit. At least, that's how I feel."

"Do the honor and glory of the kingship, without the hazard of execution, not beguile you?"

Jorian shook his head. "Had I never experienced it, it might. But for five years I had my fill of donning ornate costumes, and sitting through tedious ceremonies, and hearing the lying arguments of litigants and petitioners, and trying to collect enough taxes to keep the kingdom going without inciting a revolt. So tell your people I am flattered but firm in my refusal."

"But think of all the good you could accomplish!"

Jorian smiled. "That's the excuse every tyrant gives in snatching at total power. But from what I've seen of the world, plans to better the lot of the people seldom turn out as the planners hope, even with the best intentions."

"Will nought persuade you?"

"Nought whatever. Your legislature will have to muddle along without my wisdom."

Corineus stared at the ground. "I—I ought to thank you—I made a bit of an ass of myself on our first meeting. You—you had been justified in slaying me...."

Jorian grinned. "Forget the whole episode. When I was ten years younger, I did silly things, too. But let me ask you: How did you, an admirer of the old feudal regime, get involved in a popular revolutionary movement?"

Corineus looked embarrassed. "Forsooth, Estrildis talked me into it. She said 'twas the only way our marriage would ever be fully recognized as legal in Xylar. She can be very persuasive."

"I know," said Jorian. "How is she?"

"Fine, and so is the boy. She is getting—well, a trifle plump."

"Give her my brotherly love."

"Where is the old Mulvanian?"

"Karadur is a professor in Othomae, having compassed the ouster of his predecessor Abacarus. I had something—" Jorian was about to say "to do with that," but thought better of it. "He wants me to teach an engineering course at the Academy. What befell that clerk, Thevatas?"

"He was hanged."

"Indeed? My grief overwhelms me not. How fell it?"

"The Regency offered a generous reward for recovering the crown, but he held out for a seat on the Council. Believe it or not, he lusted to command the army. Losing patience, they feigned to agree and then, as soon as they had the royal headpiece, hustled him off to the scaffold with hardly a pretense of legal process."

"So perish overreachers!" said Jorian. "Now join me in a glass of wine, and then be off to tell the Xylarians what I have said. When one has been to as many places, and worked at as many trades, and suffered through as many vicissitudes as I have, if he have learnt nought else, he should at least know when he is well off!"

About the Author

L. Sprague de Camp, who has over ninety-five books to his credit, writes in several fields: historicals, SF, fantasy, biography, and popularizations of science. But his favorite genre of literature is fantasy.

De Camp is a master of that rare animal *humorous fantasy*. As a young writer collaborating with the late Fletcher Pratt, he set forth the world-hopping adventures of Harold Shea. These are available today in two books: *The Compleat Enchanter* and *Wall of Serpents*. Together, Pratt and de Camp also wrote the delightfully zany *Tales from Gavagan's Bar*, a book which has remained in print for forty years.

In 1976, at the 34th World Science Fiction Convention, he received *The Gandalf—Grand Master Award for Lifetime Achievement in the Field of Fantasy*. The Science Fiction Writers of America presented him with their *Grand Master Nebula Award of 1978*. Alone, and with his wife and sometime collaborator Catherine, de Camp has been a welcome guest of honor at fan conventions throughout the United States.

The de Camps live in Villanova, Pennsylvania. They have two sons: Lyman Sprague, and Gerard Beekman, both of whom are distinguished engineers.